ARCANA

Flashes of the Supernatural

SUSANA K. MARSCH

Sun Mars Impressions

For rights and permissions, please contact the author at
susanakmarsch@gmail.com

ISBN-13: 978-0-9987866-4-3

To all my family and friends who support me every
day,
Thank you.

CONTENTS

Dear Reader,

In this book, you will find a small collection of flash fiction and short stories to either chill your bones or make you smile.

These tales are a small portion of many years of gazing at Tarot cards and writing the stories they inspire.

I chose the best and dearest examples of stories inspired by the Major Arcana, though they are not in order and have few references to the Tarot. They were once published on my blog: www.susanakmarsch.com.

I have also mixed this collection with unpublished stories written over the years.

I hope you will enjoy *Arcana: Flashes of the Supernatural.*
With haunting regards,

SM

Susana K. Marsch

Arcane

Derek stood before the bookcase and sighed. He scanned the spines, searching for the book stated in his handwritten note. It did not help that the borrower had only provided the title of the book. He checked the catalog and the only reference was "occult", which had turned out to be an extensive section in the library basement. He was on his third bookcase.

Aha! Derek checked his note again and retrieved a dusty book with strange symbols on the cover and titled "Necromancy, Wizardry and Dark Magic" in big, bold letters. He sneered as he perused the pages; pure balderdash and poppycock. Utter bullshit.

He heard a strange rumble far away and wondered whether a storm was coming. Derek shrugged and tucked the book under his arm. He turned to leave when the ground shook and flung him into the bookcase. The lights flickered, and the books rattled in their shelves; a few tumbled onto the floor. When the tremor ended, Derek rubbed his shoulder and sighed. He set the requested book aside and stooped to pick up the fallen books and re-shelve them.

One lay open, and, as Derek reached for it, a cold draft blew through the aisle and flipped the pages. Derek squinted as he tried to read the writing. He did not understand the language, nor the alphabet. Something crept up his spine and tickled the back of his mind.

He sat cross-legged on the floor, and without touching the book, stared at the pages. He sensed he could almost read the writing, as if he had once known it but had forgotten long ago. The pages then turned to an illustration.

A baby in swaddling clothes left behind at a doorstep. Derek examined the picture and wondered why it brought feelings of déjà vu. A memory flashed; he sat in the kitchen with his mother, snacking on milk and cookies.

"You found me on the doorstep," he had said, matter-of-fact.

"Of course not," his mother had smiled, "you were born in the hospital. I know, I was there."

The memory ended, and his mind focused on the picture. Though he could not see it, he knew the doorstep belonged to an earthen home with people around a warming fire.

The picture moved, and Derek, frightened yet curious, wondered whether his mind was tricking him. The door creaked open; an old woman peeked out. She saw the baby, picked it up, gazed left and right, and cradling it, took it inside the hut. Derek's heart thumped as long-forgotten dreams flared and burst into puffs of haze in his mind. Could he be the baby?

"Derek! Are you down there?"

The boss's voice plunged into the basement and broke the spell. Only the strange writing remained on the page.

"Coming!" He yelled.

Derek closed the book; the cover was old, leather-bound, weather-beaten and title-less. He put it back on the shelf, at the very end where no one would notice it. He grabbed the book on magical crapola and walked toward the stairs, reluctant to climb them.

The library closed and Derek, the last to leave, snuck down to the occult section, retrieved the book, hid it under his jacket, and took it home.

Moonlight shone as he pulled into the driveway, its eerie silvery light an omen, which Derek felt with every cell in his body.

"Once in a blue moon, Derek," Grandpa's forgotten voice whispered in his memory, "a book comes along that changes your life."

Mesquite

The scraggly mesquite tree creaked in the soft breeze blowing through the open window and billowing the voile curtains.

"It's a peculiar tree," the hired arborist had told Daisy and Paul, "It's at least one-hundred-and-fifty years old, and though bare, it's very much alive and healthy. It has no plague or disease, yet, you say it doesn't regrow its leaves?"

Daisy nodded, "We bought the house at least three years ago, and we've never seen a blossom or a leaf on that tree. I love how its twisted branches spread out like a bony canopy."

Paul shrugged, but the expert had agreed.

"Yes'm, there's a certain melancholic beauty to it. My advice: enjoy its spidery shade, there's life in the old dog yet."

Though the sun shone and the cool breeze blew through the backyard, Daisy and Paul spent the morning in the living room, measuring spaces and pondering whether a new oaken sideboard would fit under the windows that looked out at the tree.

Paul raised his cellphone to his face, "Let's see if this A.R. app works."

"A.R.?" asked Daisy.

"Augmented reality," he answered, "it can overlay a picture of the sideboard we want onto our room, so we can see if it fits before we buy it."

Daisy nodded, impressed. She glanced over Paul's shoulder as he pointed the cellphone camera at the windows. She smiled when the image of the sideboard appeared in her living room while the skeletal branches of her beloved tree peeked through the frame.

Paul said, "I think it would look good, don't you?"

And Daisy was about to agree when she noticed a shadow pass over the image.

"What's that?"

Paul turned his eyes back to the phone screen. In it, the living room walls disappeared, and the tree stood in leafy pomp, outlined by a blazing firmament.

"Huh," Paul muttered, and lifted his eyes from the screen.

The warm, yellow sunshine of midday poured through the windows and onto the gray-green vinyl-plank floor, reflecting off the cream-colored walls. On the phone screen, the tree stood on a lonely grassland beneath a fiery red sky.

"It is the same tree," Daisy said, "I know every tangled bough, but it's blooming!"

The screen flickered, and silhouettes approached the tree. The couple distinguished a group of rough-and-tumble men on horseback. A man with arms tied behind his back stumbled behind them as one rider pulled him along by a rope.

"It's a posse!" Paul exclaimed, and they watched transfixed as it reached the tree.

One man slung a noose over a high branch. The others pulled the tethered man forward and placed the noose around his neck. Then, they tugged on the rope, and the bound man flew upwards.

The laughing and cheering bandits tied the rope to the tree trunk, while the hanged man dangled and jerked from the noose.

The sun dipped on the horizon; the hanged man grew still and swung back and forth. The posse mounted their horses and rode away. The sun shot out its last rays over the empty grassland, and twilight settled over the extinguished life. A mournful wind howled and wailed, blowing away all the leaves from the hanging tree.

The Old Library

Joan paced the Old Library, checking everything was in place. This branch housed only the history and genealogy resources of the Main Library two streets away. The building was a Post-Medieval English New England house with a plaque claiming it as the town's oldest structure. At least three hundred years old, and though a private residence for generations, the last descendants had willed it to the town upon their deaths.

Joan often pondered about the downfall of the old families as she sat at the circulation desk, sometimes playing solitaire on the computer. Never the busiest of branches, most patrons—except for the members of the local historical society—only stopped to gape at the ancient building.

Evening was falling upon the shelves on her first closing up since Joan's recent transfer to this branch. Betty, her boss, went home early with an upset stomach.

The library boasted one central chimney flanked by two rooms, known as the hall and the parlor. Upstairs, in the garret, one of two tiny bedrooms functioned as a study room available to patrons, the other was the staff break room.

A long lane wound around the building and dead-ended at the town's majestic Georgian style Wells House, now a museum. It and the Old Library had belonged to the Wells, the oldest and wealthiest family in town. They built the mansion as their wealth grew and vacated the much older family home, using it first as a groundskeeper cottage, then left abandoned with their demise. The Wells died out decades ago, their fortune depleted.

Joan peeked through the small, diamond-paned casement window. Flurries fluttered about the dusky night. She glanced at her watch, still an hour to go before closing time. She meandered to the old stone fireplace and sat down on one of the cozy high-backed chairs facing it. Poking the dying fire, the embers sparkled and twirled upon the now coal-black log. Joan wondered whether to rekindle it, but, even in its last flickers, the fire emitted enough cozy heat. Dim sconces lit up the rooms, and far from eerie, they produced a special welcoming warmth.

Above the fireplace hung the portrait of a lady dressed in 18th century garb with her hair teased and curled into a pompadour. She wore a red dress with frilled cuffs, low neckline and tight corset. Joan thought her a plain woman of a certain age, dressed in the wealthy finery of a young girl. The portrait needed restoration; the background had darkened to indiscernible murkiness and cracks showed on the woman's serious face. Her marble chest, devoid of ornaments, was the brightest spot on the portrait.

Joan sat and gazed, and for the first time, noticed the woman's desolate expression. A lump caught in Joan's throat as she beheld the saddened eyes sunken into the pallid face. Her thin lips pulled downward in utter misery.

On Joan's first day at the Old Library, Betty had explained the portrait's history. Joan had only half-listened as she pondered the odd placement of the picture. Shouldn't it hang in the Wells House Museum instead? The high, elaborate hairdo and elegant clothing contrasted with the low ceilings and barebones style of the Old Library.

Blue shadows of twilight criss-crossed the walls. The fire sputtered, and the ensuing flicker illuminated the painted lips with a ghostly quiver.

If only Joan could remember the story.

Was she courted by a prince? No, that was her ancestor.

Joan's memory clicked into place.

And the prince had gifted the ancestor a precious diamond necklace, which she'd passed down the line to this woman, who had…

Joan scrunched her face and considered phoning Betty, but thought better of it; she went home green with nausea.

Let's see, as a young girl the lady in the portrait had…

Had an affair with a British soldier during the Revolution!

Yes, but first, the necklace had disappeared. Then, someone had betrayed the lovers as they tried to elope and accused the soldier of stealing the necklace. She defended him, but the community shamed and shunned her and…

What happened? He died in battle?

No, he hanged for theft, though the necklace never appeared. And…

A pariah, she lived in squalor in this building for the rest of her life.

A draft of air blew and sparked the glowing embers of the fireplace. Smoke and ash scattered everywhere, and Joan coughed and wheezed until the ash settled on the wooden floor by the high-backed chair.

As the smoke cleared, Joan glimpsed ash seeping through the cracks, delineating one, and only one wooden plank. She kneeled down and, running her fingers over it, realized she could hook her pinky nail under it and pry it loose.

Cautious and praying no rodent bit her, Joan stuck her hand into the gaping rectangle. Her fingers clasped around cloth. She pulled out a bundle of worn fabric and unwrapped it.

Her hands shone with bejeweled diamonds woven into a gold chain. She held it to the light, marveling as the stones caught the beams and reflected them back into the dim library.

"I believe that belongs to me," the voice of a young woman whispered and Joan turned towards the sound.

The portrait gazed down at her. A painted arm moved and reached through the turbid varnish of the picture and out into the room, so close it almost touched Joan's face.

The woman held her arm out, palm up, expecting Joan to place the necklace on it. Shuddering, Joan deposited the jewels in the outstretched fingers.

"Thank you," the woman said, smiling.

Another gust howled through the library. Twinkling embers danced around the portrait of the smiling young girl in wealthy dress and pompadour hairstyle with a shining necklace draped around her neck. A handsome man in a tricorn hat beamed behind her.

Mind Full

"This is stupid," Edith wriggled in her lotus position. She moved her neck from side to side and straightened her shoulders. With a deep breath, she tried to focus on the yoga instructor's soft, lulling voice as he led the class into a meditation.

Edith wondered why she was here. Her therapist had recommended yoga for stress management and, like a fool, she had obliged. The guy next to her squirmed and the rustle of his movement sounded like nails on a chalkboard. Someone behind her cleared their throat, and that too grated at her brain.

Edith inhaled again, forcing herself to focus, but the instructor's words meant nothing. Her never-ending to-do list occupied her thoughts.

Darkness surrounded her through her closed eyes; someone must have turned off the lights. She had not realized how much the yellow light filtering through her eyelids bothered her. Then something clicked in Edith's brain and muted the anxious thoughts. She felt herself melt into the ground as she exhaled.

She was in utter darkness now and frightened, as she sensed her arms go limp and her shoulders droop, but the soft chanting seeped through the blackness and calmed her.

It grew louder until she distinguished the low, yet mellifluous unison of men's voices intoning unintelligible words. The perfect harmony of their singing suggested to Edith she might be inside a temple or a church. The sound echoed inside a vault, though the yoga studio had a low ceiling.

A shudder, no, a trickle crept up her fingertips and a warm electricity coursed through her. Not a jolt, but a sense of home.

A point of light appeared in the darkness that clouded Edith's mind. It merged with the blackness and she glimpsed a simple altar, made of rough-hewn wood and stone, unlike the one she had seen that time in the cathedral.

The point of light expanded and a procession of hooded men walked in front of her. They made the lovely music with their voices. Aware she walked among them, Edith peeked at the monk beside her, but his cowl draped too far over his forehead and she only glimpsed an aquiline nose.

Edith gazed at her hands, and startled when she saw the thick palms, heavy fingers, and wrinkled skin that clung onto the bone. One fingernail was black and, disgusted, Edith meant to fold the finger and hide the nail. Instead, the muscle twitched and sent a bolt through her body. The chants and the monks disappeared, and she was back in the yoga studio.

The Hacienda

The humid heat blasted me as I opened the car door. The overcast sky throbbed with a dense and muffled silence, and I wondered if it would storm tonight.

The hotel receptionist greeted us with a smile. I gazed around the small reception with its plastered stone walls, modest provincial furniture, low ceilings and unmistakable scent of mildew drifting down from the wooden rafters. The old hacienda, now the best hotel in the region, offered thermal-spring swimming pools, *temazcales* and water sports on the blue-green lake.

The receptionist explained a little about the hacienda's history as he checked our reservation.

A Spanish noble built it in the sixteenth century and had been the head of a network of mining haciendas nearby.

"The family lived here," the receptionist said, "one night, lightning struck the main building, and it succumbed to fire. After a century of abandon, new owners built this space which comprises the lobby, the offices and the dining room. They never rebuilt the ruins and lived here until the family died out. Afterwards, it passed from owner to owner until the current one converted it into this hotel."

I felt his gaze on me, scrutinizing me and following my every movement, not with suspicion, but as if he recognized me. I'd never visited this place and, though I listened to his rehearsed introduction, I could not take my eyes off the portrait above the dining room entrance. A man, gray-haired, stern and ruthless, stared at me through steel-colored eyes that pierced the ancient canvas and stabbed my heart. Chills crept up my spine. I had the scary sensation I'd seen him somewhere.

"Señora, that is the *hacendado*, Don Pedro Maldonado de Alarcón. He lived here with his daughter when the hacienda caught fire."

I turned to the receptionist and caught a mischievous glint in his eyes, as if he wanted to continue, but waited for me to respond.

"Oh, yeah?" I gave him a nonchalant shrug, though that portrait captured my gaze.

"What happened to him?" My husband Frank asked, falling straight into the honey trap.

"No one knows," the receptionist narrowed his eyes, "they think he perished in the fire, but they never found his remains."

"Wow," Frank was hooked. I also enjoyed a mystery, but this time, I felt I already knew the conclusion.

"Yes, the legend says he caught his daughter eloping with the *capataz*—how you say—foreman. They say he killed them, then the lightning struck, and the fire broke out. People say it was God's punishment. Her portrait hangs in the dining room. You should see it."

He grinned at me, as if hinting something.

"Shall we go to our room?" I said, a blank smile on my face.

"You are in the Doña Pilar suite, go through that door and follow the well-marked paths. I will send the bell boy with your luggage."

We smiled and walked out into the sultry air of the cobblestone courtyard.

I gasped.

"What is it?" Frank asked.

"I've been here before," I whispered, "in dreams. You know which ones."

"Where you are trying to escape and you run down paths and courtyards?"

"Yes! And I'm running towards someone, I want to warn them, but someone's hunting me."

"Damn."

The cool breeze ululated like a crying woman through the tall, moss-laden trees of the dusky hacienda. I hugged myself while Frank glanced at the key and turned towards a path. The breeze enticed me to follow the narrow path that led to the small stream. Up ahead, I glimpsed a wall—both a dam and a narrow bridge. The gurgling stream sounded like running feet.

Thunder cracked like gunshots. In the milky light, I glimpsed a young couple shot down with each thunderclap as they hurried across the bridge. The old man in the painting stood beside me, the musket still smoking in his arms. The bodies drifted down the stream, silky red water flowing behind them. Lightning flashed as they passed me, her in a heavy purple dress and corset, him in breeches, boots and shirt. I gazed into the woman's face. My heart jolted; she looked like me!

Gasping, I glanced away.

The old man was gone.

Though I heard the faint cry of *"fuego!"*, nothing was amiss.

Adulting

Rick slid the chain-lock into place and scanned his apartment; his first adult home. The rent was nothing to laugh at, but satisfaction glowed out of his eyes as he surveyed his new domain. Several boxes stood open against the wall, and tomorrow he would rent a U-Haul and pick up the secondhand dining set he had bought online. Though small, his apartment was perfect; top story on a separate wing with no next-door or upstairs neighbors, except for the empty unit below his. A new pre-owned car and exciting new job; his best years had begun.

Rick padded to the bedroom and turned off all the lights. His parents always complained he wasted electricity. But now, with a brand new contract in his name and linked to his credit card, Rick was very conscious of the value of energy.

He climbed into bed and turned off the lamp. He stared at the ceiling, zigzagged by the shadows of the busy city as moving cars left a wake of light beams across it. His eyelids drooped, and he was drifting into sleep when the voice whispered.

"How should we do it?"

The voice, female, young and high-pitched, was so close in his ear his eyes flew open. His heart jumped to his throat, pumping blood so fast he thought it would leap out of his chest.

"We could smother him in his sleep," another female voice, older and hoarse, replied.

Trembling, Rick reached for the switch; the room flooded with light. He sat up in bed. Everything was as he had left it. Only…

He had draped his pants over the plastic patio chair furnishing the room. They now lay in a heap on the floor beside it.

Rick slid out of bed and tiptoed to the window. City lights shone in full splendor; a foghorn blew in the distance. He crept across the room towards the door, cursing himself for leaving his baseball bat in the car. He peeked into the adjacent bathroom. Nothing out of place. He then made his cautious and frightened way through the tiny apartment. Nothing wrong; locked deadbolt and the chain crossed the door.

Satisfied he was alone, Rick grabbed the cutter he used to open the boxes and returned to bed. He flicked off the light and listened. Street sounds. He calmed down and closed his eyes.

"We could also poison him," the youthful voice whispered.

Rick sat up and switched on the light.

"No," the older voice spoke, and Rick pressed himself against the wall, knees to his chest.

The voices were in the room, but he saw no one.

"If we smother him, it would seem like he died in his sleep."

"How do we get rid of the body?"

"We don't, we make a big deal about finding him."

Rick listened to the disembodied conversation, frozen with fear.

Headlights traced their way across the ceiling. Car doors closed, footsteps on the concrete.

"He's here," the younger voice said.

Rick forced his body to the window. He tried to gaze down into the street, but the fire escape blocked his view of the parking lot.

He listened for sounds in the hall; his ears caught the click of a doorway and footsteps crossing the apartment below him. Rick slunk back into bed and drew the covers up to his chin, pondering whether to call the police.

Then he remembered the realtor had said the apartment below remained unoccupied. The last tenant, he said, had died in his sleep years ago. The widow and daughter had moved out soon afterwards.

The Man on the Street

The man just started playing with the child's toys. I thought it odd and out of the ordinary. The way he sat down at the table and started playing with the boy's truck seemed so out of place it moved me, gave me an unusual feeling that something wasn't right.

What is it? I thought, what's off about this picture? And then I realized the boy's father, sitting next to the child, and pretending to play with him while engrossed in his phone, took no notice at all. He never lifted his head when the man pulled out one of the remaining two chairs and sat at their table. The boy seemed unperturbed that someone grabbed his truck and was wheeling it all over the tabletop. Do they know him? Is the man a friend or a relative?

I had seen the man walking by the tables on the sidewalk patio. He sauntered by once or twice, not in a hurry, as if window shopping. He seemed wealthy, maybe in his sixties or seventies, with a tailored three-piece gray suit and black woolen flat cap. He didn't stand out in the crowd of city-dwellers walking by, but something about him caught my attention and I couldn't put my finger on it. He seemed calm and collected, and unhurried, like many men his age.

I scrutinized his demeanor and his appearance. He had a kind face underneath the cap, and he smiled and laughed as he zigzagged the toy truck around the table. His clothing was neat and ironed, and I thought I caught a whiff of a musky eau-de-toilette wafting towards me. The gray suit had a herringbone pattern, which shimmered in the silvery light, and I thought he must have been dashing in his youth. Then I noticed his shoes, the polished black tips glimmering from beneath spotless spats of such a brilliant white they hurt my eyes. No one wears spatterdashes anymore. Clouds blotted out the sun, and a draft of cold air blew from the strange man playing with the toy truck; an eerie chill crawled over my skin.

I searched for the waiter, my finger in the air to get his attention. He was flitting around the tables, taking orders, filling water glasses. The restaurant was packed and the hubbub of conversation mingled with the honking and zoom of the street traffic. The father and son still paid no attention to the man. The boy gazed at his toys with a bemused grin, grasping a toy car with one hand, while the other lay flat with fingers splayed on the table.

"Miss? May I get you something?" the waiter appeared beside me.

"Um, yes, I..."

I turned to point at the strange man, but a shaft of sunlight shone on his empty chair, and the little boy was gazing at me with wide-eyed confusion.

Cloudburst

He came into my life like storm clouds rolling down a mountain. A tranquil afternoon at a café window, distant rumble, occasional flashes and then he was upon me. He dazzled me with his windswept hair and sunbathed skin as he stood over me, smiling, asking if I was using the empty chair across from me. No, I said and smiled. He cocked his head and with a devilish grin he lifted the chair and placed it before the adjacent table, facing me.

Soon after, I floated on the silver clouds of love and infatuation. Summer days, sultry nights, and always that distant thunder. I let the balmy passion which fogs the brain and blinds the eye wash over me, envelop me and pull me into the eerie calmness at the center. Joyful times in the storm's eye.

Joyful times gone too soon.

First, he sprinkled questions here and there. Though I knew I owed him no answers, I still explained. He required explanations.

Then, the torrent of accusations, dense with jealousy, engulfed me and I swirled in the gale of his obsession. I flailed and grasped at the gusting wreckage of my life. I tried to clasp onto friends and family whirling around me, but he held on strong and my grip slipped.

I would love to say I made it through the tempest, kept my head down and turned my collar up against the wind. I want to say I laughed at the lightning and roared louder than the thunder; but no, he vanished as he had come; in a blinding flash.

Now, all I have left is my name on a gravestone.

The Ancient Cemetery

The forest had swallowed the ancient cemetery until all that remained was the stone angel projecting from the undergrowth. The name on the tomb had vanished and moss and dead leaves covered the statue's feet. Lichen clung to its wings. Twining plants wound and twirled around the statue's legs, and Spanish moss hung from its outstretched arms. The right hand clutched a sword ready to strike. The left hand held an uneven balance scale with empty pans, their weights lost in the sands of time. A thin mist always hovered as a ghostly reminder of the long-forgotten names interred there.

Miranda and Maureen had visited this place since their youth; the twin sisters loved to meander around the mounds of earth, moss and protruding partial headstones. They loved to gaze at the stone angel with facial features smoothed out by time and the encroaching forest. Tall trees surrounded the burial grove and a break in the topmost branches allowed a tiny ray of sun to shine its feeble light on the statue. For decades, every Saturday, the sisters had taken the narrow and nigh invisible path to the ancient graves. Then had sat on a rock before the stone angel to enjoy a picnic of sandwiches, chips and soda.

Birds trilled in the trees as Miranda traipsed through the path, broken and uneven by the thick roots of the tall oaks that lined it. Once Miranda approached the grove, all sound ceased and the perennial thin mist hung low about the ground. Here she found the solace and comfort she needed from the oppressive burden of loss. She missed her twin sister's following footsteps and sometimes felt the warmth of her body beside her. But when she turned her head, Miranda saw only the rainbow caused by the feeble sunlight through the spectral mist.

Miranda sat on the rock and wept. Maureen would never visit this place again; those happy picnics gone forever, ripped from her by a careless teenager from the prestigious boarding school on the outskirts of town and his fancy fast car. Miranda took out a black-and-white picture of the sisters in their younger days with their beehive hairstyle, strapless gowns, and coy smiles. In their prom picture, Miranda and Maureen were as young as the boy with the flying red car who had plunged Miranda into a life of one.

"The sign flashed 'walk' and he didn't stop! Oh, Maureen!" Miranda cried, and her voice broke the eerie silence. Her blood boiled as she recalled the police dropping the charges the moment the boy's father had opened his checkbook. An unfortunate accident they ruled.

Now, the ritual comprised tears over a fresh grave in a proper cemetery, then a melancholy picnic before the stone angel. The boy zoomed past her as Miranda left the graveyard. She walked through the town center on her way to the forest; the bright red car parked on the street. The boy and his friends sat at a cafe's outdoor patio, laughing and joking, not for one moment heeding the sad old woman with the quivering lips. Miranda hung her head and, with leaden steps, trudged to the ancient burial ground and its funereal serenity.

On the rock, Miranda put her face in her hands and sobbed, her wails shaking the tree leaves, yet muffled by the mist.

"Justice! What justice is that?" She lamented.

"Miranda," a voice whispered and startled Miranda.

The trees rattled, and a figure emerged from the statue. First the feet surfaced, then the tunic and the arms with the scale and sword. The face took on radiant and benevolent features and at last, the pearly glimmering wings materialized.

The angel stood before Miranda and smiled. He showed her the balance scale. On the heavy plate, she saw an image of her sister's grave, while on the lighter plate the image of the rich boy appeared. He was at the café, as she had seen him moments before, still laughing and joking.

The angel swung the sword and Miranda smelled the metal as it swooped by her. The plate with her sister's grave rose while the other lowered. The scale clicked into place.

Miranda watched the principal expel the boy from school.

The scale tipped and the once-generous, over-protective father threw the boy from his house.

Again, the scale clicked into place and the boy, with blood-shot eyes and tattered clothing, stood on a street corner and leaned into the window of a black car.

With each tip of the scale, the boy became a man. By the seventh click, he was homeless and freezing in the driving snow of an unnamed street; the scales almost balanced.

Miranda watched with bated breath as the scale tipped one last time. The homeless man stood on a street corner. The 'walk' sign flashed; he stepped off the curb. A bright red streak hit him. The speeding car did not stop for the vagrant dying on the street.

The plates leveled on the angel's balance scale, and Miranda's eyes filled with tears.

"Thank you," she whispered and wiped her eyes with her fingers.

The angel vanished, and the sun shone its single beam on the nameless grave with the stone statue. Wind gusted through the trees and lifted the oppressive sorrow from Miranda's heart.

Reflection

Jenny stared at the funhouse. Lightning flashed in the distance, yet the town fair was still in full swing. She counted her tickets, aware of her dad's impatience to be home before the storm arrived.

"It'll be a big one," Dad said and allowed Jenny one last game. She chose the funhouse.

Jenny took a deep breath and advanced toward the attendant, her tickets held out before her like a dangling paper snake.

A shy, soft-spoken child, with plain brown hair, plain brown eyes, round glasses and a tiny pinched nose, Jenny looked like a frightened squirrel. At school, kids teased and bullied her for being a weakling, a bookworm, and a doormat. At home, she listened to her centenarian grandmother's stories of the Mexican Revolution, Pancho Villa and growing up with the *soldaderas*, women, like her great-grandmother, who had taken up arms. Jenny wished she were a soldadera. Now, at the funhouse entrance, was her moment to prove her bravery to herself, because the funhouse scared her to death.

She entered and walked through the mirror maze with caution, gazing at her altered reflection. Here, tall and thin, there, squat and fat, or slanted, bent and squiggled. Jenny tried to laugh, but seeing herself amplified and deformed frightened her. She reached the center of the maze, and a circle of mirrors multiplied her into all shapes and sizes.

Jenny stood, eyes to the ground, daring herself to look at the plethora of Jennys surrounding her, when thunder clapped and the lights went out. It lasted a moment, yet Jenny's heart skipped in her chest, her stomach jumped, and she shut her eyes. An instant later, the generator whirred, and the lights turned on again. Jenny counted to three and opened her eyes.

She was still in the funhouse and surrounded by mirrors, but, instead of the multitude of Jennys, she gaped at an oncoming cavalry. Shots rumbled around her like the thunder outside until she did not know which was which.

The men on horseback wore big sombreros and, by the neckerchiefs that masked their faces, Jenny knew they were bandidos out for blood and pillage. Screams soon mixed with the thunder and gunfire; someone shouted at Jenny in her grandmother's Spanish and she turned in the direction.

In the mirror beside her stood a young woman in a long blue skirt, high-necked blouse, and her plain brown hair wrapped into a bun. She gazed at Jenny through her plain brown eyes and round glasses upon her tiny pinched nose. In her arms, the woman held a rifle, and slung across her torso, she wore a bandolier, replete with ammunition. The woman nodded at Jenny, who felt the weight and cold metal of the gun in her own hands.

The woman fixed her eye on one bandido and fired. Jenny staggered back from the recoil; the rifle hot, yet safe in her arms. Jenny, together with the woman in the mirror, lifted the gun to her shoulder, fixed her sight on another bandido and shot. Again and again, they fired. One by one, the bandidos fell, and in doing so, their image in the mirrors disappeared until only the young soldadera and Jenny remained.

The soldadera set her rifle down and Jenny felt her arms lighten. She pierced Jenny with her plain eyes, now full of fire, then smiled and winked. She disappeared and left Jenny looking at her own self in the mirror, surrounded only by plain, distorted Jennys.

Jenny straightened herself and smiled, no longer the frightened squirrel.

I Started a Lie

Sheilah glanced around her bedroom as tears sprung to her eyes. She pinpointed the moment her world crashed. It all started with a fib; a little white lie, a lie of omission.

Sheilah turned on the radio, no longer able to bear the silence. The Bee Gees sang "I Started a Joke", and the song hit her; it chided her. Disgusted with it, and herself, she turned it off and silenced the shaming tune.

She started no joke. She had stayed silent, then uttered a fib, which snowballed into a monstrous lie. Before she knew it, she was standing in the ring of fire caused by it.

The shame smoldered in her mind and stung the back of her eyes as more tears welled up and ran down her cheeks, like liquid smoke. Her ears burned and her chest rattled from the raging force of the lie.

If only I had shut the fuck up, she thought.

But 'if only' was too late. 'If only' was a dead wish in a dried up wishing well. That fib, that little innocent lie, why did she say it?

Even now, as she replayed the events leading up to that moment, as she lived with the consequences, she could not say what possessed her to fib.

The school expelled an innocent person. A person, a friend, unable to afford a permanent record tarnished by such a disgraceful expulsion.

Sheilah tried to fix it, to no avail. Those once unspoken words now boomed louder than her voice, which dissipated like ashes in the space between her and the school principal.

"I was afraid," she said for the first time.

The realization smacked her right in the chest: fear had made her lie.

But fear of what?

"Fear of these very consequences," she said.

The silent bedroom replied with more silence until her sobs broke through it.

Sheilah lay down on the floor, rolled herself into a ball, and cried. The day turned to dusk, and night soon spilled its inky darkness over the world, and still Sheilah cried. The room darkened around her, but she noticed nothing.

"Sheilah," a voice whispered, and Sheilah opened her salt-rimmed eyes.

"Sheilah," the voice said again.

"Who is it?"

"You can still make it right," the voice whispered. It pealed like heavenly bells.

"How?"

"Tell the truth," the voice said, and a loving touch warmed her shoulder, yet she saw no one.

"It's too late!"

"No, it's never too late to be truthful. Come, I will guide you. But first, I must apologize. I wasn't there when you needed me, and this is the result."

"Who are you?"

"You know me, I appear in adversity, and I am here now."

Sheilah felt a soft kiss on her cheeks and arms that pulled her off the floor. In a daze, she grabbed her backpack, which held the crumpled, evidential truth. The loving, invisible fingers closed around her hand and guided her out the door. A resolute warmth flowed through her skin and into her tingling spine.

"Come now, let's make it right," the mellifluous voice sang in her ear.

"But who are you?"

"I am Courage."

Minutes to Midnight

<u>Evening:</u>

Luke checks into the hotel and, as the receptionist runs his credit card, he notices the photograph displayed in the lobby. It is a black-and-white photo of the majestic Victorian building. He cannot say why, but it gives him the creepy-crawlies.

"That picture was taken when the hotel opened in the 1890s," the receptionist says and hands him a key.

Luke enters his room and jolts at the sight of the black-and-white photograph hanging above the bed:

•   Art nouveau four-poster bed, nightstand, table and chair at back of room, heavy dark drapes line French doors to balcony. Sunlight gleams on bedspread.

The sleek curves of the Art nouveau style warp the mood of the photograph and gives it a bizarre, off-kilter feel.

The furniture in Luke's room is different and modern, but the layout is the same. White bedspread, blue curtains.

"It's this very room," he exclaims.

Luke shudders.

He startles at the knock; the bellboy enters with Luke's luggage and leaves.

Luke steps onto the balcony and enjoys the setting sun's milky glimmer over the cityscape.

<u>Dusk:</u>

Luke's eyes adjust as he enters from the balcony. Long shadows play upon the walls and blue imbues the room. Luke reaches for his jacket and stares at the photograph.

•   Man lies on bed, in slacks, vest and shirt, tie unfolded, legs extended on bedspread, arms behind head; resting. Face gazes towards balcony. Suit-jacket draped on chair, hat on table, shoes by bed.

Trembling, Luke grabs his wallet and hastens to the door. He leaves for dinner.

<u>Night:</u>

Luke opens the door and flicks on the light. The lamp on the nightstand is dim, but moonlight enters from the balcony. He places the keys on the nightstand and undoes his tie, preparing for bed.

His heart skips when he glimpses the photograph:

•   Man, now in striped pajamas, opens bedspread. Face blurred by light from Tiffany lamp on nightstand.

Luke gulps and wonders whether to change rooms. He phones the lobby, but no other rooms are available for the night.

"Tomorrow," the receptionist says.

Luke enters the bathroom.

<u>11:58 pm:</u>

Luke opens the bed and is about to climb in when he stops and stares at the photograph.

•   Darkened room lit by moonlight from balcony. Table and chair in silhouette, nightstand in shadow, billowing drapes. Outline of man laying on side, face towards balcony, flat sheet and blanket pulled up to neck, bedspread rolled at feet; asleep.

<u>11:59 pm:</u>

Luke stands with arms hanging and mouth open, mesmerized. His heart pounds and he gapes at the photograph.

- Woman stands at foot of bed. Long dress and tight jacket, heeled boots, corset and bustle. Hair in bun, tilted cap on head. Face blurry but turned toward sleeping man. Woman extends arm and points gun at sleeping man. Gun glitters in moonlight.

Luke's frenzied mind searches for an explanation and finds none. He wants to turn away, but cannot.

<u>Midnight:</u>

- Flash of light at gun barrel.

Luke hears a faded pop, as if from a gramophone. The light in his room dims, then brightens.

- Blanked out image, dark edges. Overexposed?

Luke screams as red spots appear and expand, soaking the white satin pillow on his bed.

The stairs

Hattie glanced upwards the stairs and sighed; their steepness was insurmountable to Hattie in her old age, though she conquered them every day. She clung on to the wooden railing and, hitching up her long skirt, started her ascent with a Herculean effort. Hattie could not fathom how today's girls in their full skirts—bell-shaped by cumbersome crinoline hoops—glided up and down stairs like fairies. Much too old for current fashions, she longed for the long dresses and high waistlines of her youth.

Up, up, up she went, taking her time, step-by-step, the wood beneath her feet creaking as loud as her old, old bones. But the steep, polished staircase did not deter Hattie. She rested when she needed and, with enormous patience and willpower, little by little she vanquished the stairs.

She paused halfway up, her hand tight around the railing, her heart pumping fast in her chest.

A scuffle, a slam, a gunshot.

The door on the top landing burst open. Two men clad in mismatched three-piece suits and newsboy caps ran out. Their feet clattered on the rickety staircase as they barreled down it. Police sirens blared in the distance as the man in pin-striped slacks flung a revolver into the gloomy alley beside the building.

The rascals reached the street and ran with footsteps clanging on the concrete sidewalk. The pin-striped man rounded a corner when his partner, who donned a plaid blue cap, stopped and glanced back at the old stairs with a mystified expression.

Pin-Stripes urged him to run, "Let's go!"

"I think I just saw her," Plaid Cap said.

Pin-Stripes paused, bouncing on his heels, unsure whether to stay or go.

Curiosity won, "Saw who?"

"The old lady. The one on the stairs."

Pin-Stripes chuckled, "Nah, that's just a ghost story. She doesn't exist. Come on!"

A Verizon van zoomed past them and splashed the sidewalk with puddle water. The two gangsters shimmered in the sunlight as murky droplets showered them, then vanished before the water hit the ground.

Picture at an Exhibition

Cecilia stared at the picture of the sailing ship rocking in the waves. The galleon slanted on the water painted with thick oil-caked brushstrokes, and the full sails depicted the harsh ocean wind. Peter stood beside her; a snide remark died on his lips when he caught her far-away gaze.

"What's the matter," he asked, "don't tell me you like this painting?"

"Well, it has so much movement," Cecilia replied, "I can almost feel the wind blowing in my face and hear the waves lapping against the boards."

"It has that," Peter conceded, "but it's just so jaded. It's about time we stopped romanticizing the pirates. They were horrible people."

"Who said anything about pirates?" Cecilia glanced at him, "There's no black flag."

"Huh…" Peter shrugged and squinted at the artwork, "must be my imagination; it's the first thing I thought."

He wandered off to gaze at the rest of exhibition.

"It's a merchant vessel," Cecilia mumbled in a monotone voice.

As she spoke, she listened to the jolly babble of sailors.

The sounds of the waves, the roaring wind, and the merry sea chanties grew louder in Cecilia's ears until she fancied herself on the keel. The gallery's marble floor rocked under her feet, though the salty air bit into her skin. She was in two places at once, inside the cool air-conditioned gallery, and aboard the watercraft.

The lookout's cry cut through the noise, "Ship! Starboard!"

An ominous gloom draped over the canvas.

Deep in the distance, Cecilia spotted sails moving fast on the waves.

"Sloop!" the lookout bellowed.

The men quieted in expectation.

The oncoming ship drew closer, dark clouds behind it, as if trying to escape a storm. Or was it bringing it? A shaft of sunlight broke through the dense clouds and glinted upon its main mast.

Cecilia covered her mouth and shrieked through her hand when something slapped down hard upon her shoulder. She jumped and whipped around in surprise.

"Jeez, I didn't mean to startle you," Peter said beside her, his hand still on her shoulder, "This picture fascinated you, didn't it?"

"You're right," Cecilia replied, fixing her frightened eyes on him, "this painting is about pirates."

An instant prior, she'd glimpsed cross-boned murder gliding upon the waves.

Fortune

What is fortune?

Many equate fortune to wealth. I learned long ago that wealth and fortune are two different things. I was fortunate in the sense I was wealthy. I had everything I wanted and even all I didn't want, and through rain, sleet or snow, at the end of my childhood, a bottomless trust fund awaited me.

Other people relate fortune to destiny and mine sprawled out before me like the red carpet before a king: college, then family business, and money, oh so much money. An easy fate for a smooth life.

The school bell rings, slicing through my reflections like my mother's knife through the pineapple upside-down cake she requested from our pastry chef for my last birthday. As kids pile into the halls, I stop and watch them, the geeks, the brains, the populars, the nerds, the dweebs, the class clowns, the drama club, the chess club and the jocks. Jason, surrounded by his rowdy buddies and spinning a football in his hand, saunters down the hallway. Jason won't get called out; Mr. Amos, the new principal, is nothing compared to the tour de force of respect Mr. Dieter commanded back then.

The school bell rings again, and the crowd dissipates, leaving the hall empty, good for silent introspection, which I seldom did, but now do nonstop. I remember the parties, the joyrides, the dates, the fun times I thought were endless…

I'm bored. I could look in on Ms. Stevenson in social studies, but I seldom attend class, though I've never lacked brains, only interest. I flitted from private school to private school until none would have me. I found contentment in a public school where I could fly by the seat of my pants and no one blinked. That was my fortunate life. Those were the days I was wild and carefree.

Mr. Gibson is a funny little man, like those yapping, nervous little dogs, and I peek into his classroom. Back turned, he's writing something on the board. I steal a glance at the students; the nerds are taking notes, the mean girls are texting and giggling, but most are trying to stay awake. Jason sits at the back, flinging spitballs at the kid in front. I don't like that kid; his name's Baxter.

Two kinds of weirdos or outcasts exist; kids who are neither here nor there. The good weirdos are hippie, artsy or kooky. They take up unusual hobbies like glassblowing or soap-carving; they smile often, keep to themselves and won't hurt a fly. Then we have the strange weirdos, the creepers, the people you wouldn't touch with a ten-foot pole. They are the ones that freeze you with their unnerving stare, never smile, say disturbing things in class, and slither down the hallway in a stench of hatred and disdain.

Baxter is a creeper. Dorian was a creeper.

I smirk when Mr. Gibson turns to the door, searching for something through the little square glass window. I bang on the door and the sound thunders through the room. Mr. Gibson jumps like a startled cat and so do the students. Jason even swallows his spitball. Mr. Gibson opens the door and peers out. His hand trembles a little and I snigger against the wall. Mr. Gibson closes the door and returns to his class. He's afraid now, and the class is nervous; spooky things happen here.

Only Baxter is unperturbed. His icy expression sends me back to the day the wheel of my fortune spun out of control.

"He'll do it, you know," Mr. Dieter whispers behind me, "Baxter is the new Dorian."

"I know," I say.

"Only a matter of time," his voice floats down the hall and into the teacher's lounge.

I know, though I wish I didn't. Nowadays I know so much more. It's ironic how I used to think I knew it all, but since my fortune changed, I now know everything; past, present and future. At the drop of a hat I knew every word, every story, every fact, the complete kit-and-caboodle. I also know every mistake. Though I encourage the kids to improve, the message doesn't always get through, and never to the Baxters or Dorians of the world.

Baxter is late today, and I know why. How do I stop so many destinies from spiraling into darkness?

I see Jason cutting class and heading out, and in him, I see myself just before my doom.

I was walking down the hall on the last days of senior year, playing hooky again, when Dorian ambled through the main entrance. He had a strange look in his eye and I thought, uh-oh.

He pointed a black hole at me. A flash of light, a boom and my luck oozed out of me in a river of gooey red on the school's linoleum floor. For the first time in my life, I shared the same fate as others, or rather, others shared my fate.

"There's still time," Mr. Dieter says beside me.

Like me, he knows everything, and we know Baxter hasn't left home yet, he's still pulling on his hunting clothes and packing the weapons: handguns, rifles, knives.

Jason is out the school door, but he's the only one.

The others gather beside me. We all know what's about to unfold.

Kismet brought Macy and Dorian together at the library, then he hunted Griffin into the supply closet.

Jonas fell by his locker.

Mrs. Moritz pushed Janice out of the way, but not fast enough to save herself.

Dorian shot Janice as she ran.

"We must do something," I say.

"What?" Janice, the science geek, says, "We are only air now."

"We can move things," Jonas, who was on the track and field team, pumps his fist.

"We can bang things," Griffin smiles (he was a drummer).

"We can pull the fire alarms," Mrs. Moritz chimes in (she taught music).

"We can cause a power outage," Macy piped up, she was in the drama club and now likes to fumble with the auditorium lights.

"We must hurry," Mr. Dieter looks at us and nods, "Baxter's coming."

Kids spill into the hallway and flow out the doors. Mr. Amos, the principal, yells for calm and order, but no one hears amidst the flickering lights, the clanging water pipes, the wailing fire alarms and slamming locker doors.

We cheer.

Only Mr. Dieter is not with us. He's messing with the traffic light at the end of the street.

Tomorrow, the newspapers will say Baxter Morgan ran a red light and perished when he collided with an oncoming dump truck. The police will speculate about the arsenal of weapons in his car.

The Monkey Bars

Danny loved the monkey bars. Every day at recess, he would climb on them, then cross them back and forth with his feet dangling and only the strength of his arms. His favorite part was to hook his knees on the crossbars and let himself hang upside down.

The world looked very different upside-down. He recognized his classmates, but it always took him a moment, and he thought it strange how the bullies and meanies seemed nice and the pretty girls turned ugly. Maybe the upside-down shows you the opposite of what is, thought Danny, or maybe it shows you the truth.

Danny would hang until the recess monitor demanded he right himself, or until the blood rushed to his head and his brain thumped. He feared the throb which the latter produced because it blurred his vision and muffled his hearing, almost like being underwater.

Robbie bet him he couldn't hang all recess. Danny knew the headache would come before the end, but for Robbie's cupcake, he'd do it.

The recess bell rang, and the boys beelined for the monkey bars. They glanced towards the monitor and smirked. Mr. Stanford was on duty; he was old, and he liked to sit on a bench with his eyes closed.

"I'm not sleeping, I'm just gazing inside myself," he would say, "and if you bother those girls again, you're off to detention faster than you can say 'Jack Robinson'."

The offending party would slink away, perplexed at Mr. Stanford's uncanny perspicacity.

Danny climbed on the monkey bars, crossed to the middle, lifted his legs, and hooked his knees and ankles on the crossbars.

Robbie counted down, "Three … two… one!"

Danny lowered his head and gazed at the dirt beneath him; a butterfly flitted by and alighted on a pebble. Robbie's smiling face seemed like a happy frown.

Soon, his cheeks puffed up and the first throb announced itself. He couldn't swallow and his ears got hotter and hotter. Danny imagined his head blowing up like a balloon. He took a deep breath as the thumping began. Here goes. His vision clouded, and the world narrowed. At that moment, he would right himself, but for the sake of that creamy decadent cupcake…

The upside-down world turned red and tinted Robbie's dim and worried expression. Robbie moved his lips, but Danny heard nothing. Now he was underwater, suspended in the atmosphere, floating in spacc.

The ground cracked and opened. Fingers and hands dug their way out of the muddy, grassless dirt. Golden-haired ringlets emerged, followed by blue eyes and a creamy complexion. The girl frightened him; he distinguished the bone and sockets of her skull beneath her skin. Danny remembered why he hated this moment, he had seen her once before and she scared him.

The girl, dressed in a pink poodle skirt and white blouse, bobby socks and saddle shoes, smiled at him and touched him. Danny screamed. The world spun and blackened.

"Danny, wake up!" Mr. Stanford's voice came from far away.

Danny opened his eyes and focused on Robbie's and Mr. Stanford's worried expressions.

"Are you okay?" Robbie peeped.

"I saw her," Danny whispered, his voice hollow in his ears.

"Who?"

"The girl, I think she's buried here."

"Nonsense."

"I swear, Mr. Stanford, she wore a pink poofy skirt and her hair was all done up in curls and held back with a pink ribbon, like Goldilocks."

Mr. Stanford went from worried to scared, and Danny realized he knew about her.

"Grandpa told me a girl fell and broke her neck many years ago," Robbie whispered and Mr. Stanford gave a slight, almost imperceptible nod.

"Was that her?" Danny asked, but in an instant, the fright had passed and Mr. Stanford composed himself, saying nothing. He helped Danny stand and sent him to the nurse.

As Robbie led Danny away, he glanced back; Mr. Stanford leaned on the monkey bars, wiping tears from his eyes. The ghost girl stood beside him, shimmering in the hot day. She waved at Danny and vanished.

The House Told Me

The house menaced in the harsh sunlight. The yard was a barren plot of dry grass, and the broken windows looked like hollow eye-sockets.

"Isn't it amazing?" Katie giggled and bounced on her toes.

"Um…" I tried to stammer out a supporting response but couldn't, for the life of me, fathom why anyone would buy this house.

"It's my first fixer-upper," she squealed with delight, "it's got real potential and I think we can turn a profit."

"Does Oscar agree?" I asked, knowing my sister's penchant for pies in the sky.

"You bet!" She said and beckoned me to follow her.

I stared at the hideous building. It didn't have the charm of a bygone architectural style; square, dilapidated and bleak, it left me speechless.

"Let me show you," Katie took my hand and hurried me across the arid yard.

Charm and beauty weren't on the inside, either. We entered a box with low ceilings and no decorative features. Debris lay strewn about on the floor, lost and mismatched objects, broken glass and, in the corner, a creepy doll slumped against the wall.

My heart skipped a beat when I beheld it. Only a bare rag of what may have been an apron covered the doll. Its arm was scorched black, and it had a missing eye. Someone had pulled out most of its hair. To whom had this toy belonged?

"Do you know who lives here?" I asked Katie, unable to peel my eyes off the unfortunate doll.

"Um, no, it's abandoned." Katie answered, oblivious to the anxiety in my voice.

I cast one last look around the room as she led me towards the stairs. Eerie warped sunlight entered the window, and for the first time, I noticed the walls. My heart raced as my mind sought an explanation for the reddish brown spatters and streaks that lined the shabby wallpaper. What could have done this? These stains peppered every wall, and though they didn't look like blood, I had the strange sensation they pointed to something.

"Elise!" Katie called from the upstairs landing.

Reluctantly, I climbed the stairs that creaked and cracked under my feet. Katie stood at the top, arms akimbo, waiting for me as I dawdled. Shadows danced on the walls and ceiling behind her. I paused. Were they the distorted shapes of children?

I gulped. My mind was playing tricks on me, or was it?

I reached the top of the stairs and entered the gloomy and messy second floor.

"It doesn't have the greatest view," Katie chatted as we crept down the hallway, "but we'll figure something out."

We entered one of the smaller bedrooms. I gasped and held back a scream.

"What?" Katie asked.

"Who lived here?" I breathed.

She followed my gaze and shrugged.

"So the windows have bars," she stated with that annoying nonchalance that often made me want to punch her.

"On the inside?" I exclaimed and pointed at the iron bars that ran from the ceiling to the floor.

"Why not?" She shrugged; I gave her an annoyed glance.

A draft blew in this dreary, ugly house and sent a chill up my spine. I whipped around, certain I'd heard a child's whimper in that gust of air. Out of the corner of my eye, I saw a shadow run into the adjacent door, but I didn't dare look. Instead, I invited Katie to lunch, the sooner to hightail it without hurting her feelings. She was so damn sensitive and so eager for this horrible house any objection would fall on deaf ears.

As we turned to go, I glanced down the hall towards the master bedroom. In the fuzzy sunlight streaked on the wall, I saw, just for a moment, the dangling silhouette of a hanging man. I hurried my sister along and sped through the ground floor and its stained walls and into the dead yard.

This house is dead, but the shadows live. The words pounded in my brain and it took me a while to compose myself. Katie never noticed.

"I've heard some stories," Oscar whispered when I voiced my concern over the telephone the next day, "I heard the last owner, decades ago, hanged himself in a bedroom. They said he was heartbroken when his wife ran off with their kids."

I said no more; in the background, Katie's excited voice mixed with the rattle and boom of heavy machinery.

I hung up and went about my day, trying, and failing, to get that house out of my mind. Oscar's story rang true, but there was something…

Night fell; the phone rang.

"Oh my God, Elise!" Katie yelled before I could say the customary hello.

"What? What's happened?" I said alarmed.

"You won't believe what the workers found!"

"The skeletons of a woman and children entombed in the stained walls," I blurted out.

A pause.

"How did you know?"

"The house told me…"

Waiting

"Can I get you something else?" The waiter asked, his expression full of sympathy, yet amused. I'd been at the table for almost an hour and Kyle hadn't yet arrived. The restaurant boasted a century of continued service.

"More water, please," I smiled.

I glanced at my wristwatch. Kyle is often late, but he's never stood me up; he's my brother, I know what to expect.

I gazed out the big floor-to-ceiling window and watched the people and cars zipping by in the rush-hour bustle.

My cell phone lay on the table, by the dim Tiffany stained-glass table lamp lit up in hues of reds, greens, yellows and blues. My eyes darted from the window to the phone's dark screen. No news is good news, I thought.

A brand new 1920s black Cadillac stopped in front of the restaurant. I frowned, confused. Something felt odd about the car, its shiny newness seemed real, not like the restored hot-rods at the antique car shows Kyle likes.

The doors opened. Two men jumped out. They wore three-piece suits, one dressed in gray, the other in a pinstriped navy blue. Their hats hung low on their heads. My heart raced as they pulled out a submachine gun each.

They stood legs apart, pointed the guns at the window and fired. I heard the rat-tat-tat of the machine guns, and saw them blazing, yet the glass remained intact. No one on the street screamed or ducked; no one in the restaurant panicked. In the line of fire, I was unscathed.

The men climbed in the car and sped away.

Was I dreaming? A car honked somewhere and brought the restaurant itself back to reality.

I glanced around, wondering whether others had seen the gangsters. For the first time, I noticed a line of bullet holes in the back wall, gaping in the ancient and faded wallpaper. These were not recent, but no one had bothered to cover them.

"Hi, so sorry I'm late," Kyle slid into the chair; he was flushed and sweaty and out of breath, "what did I miss?"

"Al Capone's gang just shot up the place."

"Wait, you saw them?"

"What do you mean?"

"I came here once on a date," he took a sip of my water, "I was looking at the street when an old Caddy stopped. Two old-fashioned gangsters pulled out their Tommy guns and shot at the window."

My jaw dropped.

"No one else saw a thing," he said.

Rising Tide

Death is such a heavy word, thinks Maura; the waves lap and splash around her. She sits on the rock, and the sun dips under the bleakness of her sorrow-laden heart. She wipes tears from her eyes and wishes she could turn back time.

Last week she was settling into her new life as a happy wife, and the future lay before them like a sun-bathed prairie. They had returned from their blissful honeymoon, and the world seemed to shower them with good fortune. On that day, Maura had dared to believe in a radiant forever. How she paid for her temerity!

Painful sobs erupt in her chest, and hot lava spills over her eyelids. Tears heavy with death roll down her cheeks, and she puts her head in her hands and wails. She buckles under the sorrow of a wrecked car and a husband's life ended by a drunk driver who will never experience the aftermath: a future ripped from Maura's heart. A tornado rages through her mind as the ocean licks the rock, and the surf surrounds her as the tide rises.

The sun sinks into the water, and Maura knows she must leave the spot where he proposed to her before it disappears under the waves. Even the ocean wants to take back all the happiness it brought her.

Wouldn't it be better to stay and let the sea drown her in her grief?

"No," the ocean whispers, as the waves kiss her bare feet and play on her toes, "I'll spit you back out."

And Maura knows it is only a passing fantasy in a flash of despair. She cannot leave yet. She stands up and walks inland from the beach. She pauses and gazes toward the rock as shallow waves roll over it. Placing a loving hand on her belly, she smiles; Death left her a precious gift.

The Book

65

The book burned a hole in Derek's conscience since he stole it from the library. He tried justifying his actions to himself, but the compulsion had been irresistible.

Now the book lay in the back of his closet wrapped in an old towel. He wished he could shut it out of his mind, too. The book had brought him nothing but unrest and nightmares. He would wake in a sweat, terrified of God-knows-what and always suspecting he had been dreaming something important which slipped away as his conscience woke.

Derek glanced out the window. Fog descended and with it, silence. Foggy days always made him feel suspended in time and place, disconnected from reality, the physical world hovering somewhere between the dream state and death; the ultimate peace. But not today. Today he feared the fog, as if it wanted to attack him.

Derek glanced up the stairs, his gaze beyond the landing, his mind on the book in the dark corner of the closet.

"All right," he said, "all right, I'm coming."

After much grunting and rummaging, Derek retrieved the book from its prison. He tucked it under his arm, still in its terry-cloth wrap, and brought it to the kitchen, turning on every light in the house. He unwrapped it.

The book was still in good condition; maybe if he returned it, no one would know it had left the library. He ran his fingers over the leather cover and, with a deep intake of breath, opened it.

Derek frowned, he expected to see the illustrated old cottage, but the page was blank. He flipped through the pages and his heart raced; the entire book was blank.

He was about to shut it, beads of cold sweat on his face, when a picture formed. Derek watched open-mouthed as it came to life.

A young boy stood in the forest, fractured moonlight shone through the tall trees. Dressed in a tunic and sandals, the boy trudged through dead leaves and mossy ground. He neither stumbled nor tripped, though the forest was dark; he knew the way.

The boy approached a shack, and a strange silence hung in the air. Derek's heart raced as broken images of long-ago nightmares flared in his mind. The boy, alert and uneasy, clutched a silver dagger on his belt. Something was awry, the world felt strange, and Derek urged the boy to run. The boy did not hear Derek's warning, nor did he run. Instead, he opened the ramshackle door and entered. Moonlight shone through the tiny windows and the remnants of a fire glowed in the corner. Smoke billowed into the boy's eyes; it stung Derek's eyeballs.

The darkness took shape, lumps appeared on the floor, against the walls. The room stank of blood; Derek covered his nose. The boy approached the embers and lit a torch made of stick and cloth. He bent by the nearest mass and passed the light over it. The boy jumped back. Sightless eyes and blue lips gaped up at him. He swung the makeshift torch around, the dark lumps now bloody corpses in the light.

Derek screamed and shut the book. He had known all along what the boy would find: the mangled corpses of his murdered family.

Gardenias in the Storm

My grandmother smelled like gardenias; she taught me to play chess. I sit on the window-seat and watch the stormy night, remembering the cozy evenings at the chessboard in her living room. The streetlight flickers in the driving rain. The wind howls and knocks on the windowpane; it wants to enter.

I yawn. My book lies open on my lap, awaiting me to turn the page, but I reminisce and the house heaves an exasperated sigh. I lean my forehead on the cool glass and let the memories flow. The cuckoo clock ticks, the only remnant from my grandmother's living room. Each tick-tock sends me back to my childhood, the chessboard and the constant scent of gardenias.

Cuckoo! It strikes the hour and I jolt as lightning flashes. The room lights up and for an instant, I'm sitting in Grandma's living room, the chessboard before me, the fire crackling.

"Sarah…" she whispers, but I don't see her.

The cuckoo is still chiming; twelve times it must chime.

I gaze out the window. A young woman stands in the lamplight. She looks up at me; her face aglow. I recognize Grandma, though it's the grandmother I only saw in her wedding pictures.

"Sarah…"

She smiles and waves.

I wave back.

The cuckoo slides back into its house. Rain patters against my window. I turn away. I'm back in my room on the window-seat, my book still open on my lap. I sigh; the balmy redolence of gardenias enfolds me.

Noir

The lighthouse orb carousels over the rocks, the ocean, the beach.

It rolls through the window and casts shadows on the parlor floor, the wall, the ceiling. Embers glow in the fireplace, twinkling with the swiveling ray.

The heavy pendulum clock ticks against the wall.

He sits in the armchair, still and silent.

Tick, tick, tick.

A merry-go-round, the beacon.

Light, then shadow on the gaze of steel.

Embers crackle; the sputter of an automobile rolling up the drive.

Tick, tock.

The key turns in the door; the creaking mingles with the ticking clock.

And all the while the light goes around and around in the gloom.

Moonless, starless sky.

The lighthouse sphere swirls on the placid ocean, the water like tar. Licorice fingers of lichen on the rocks. Pebbles roll with the waves upon the beach.

Tick, tock.

A footstep in the hall. The soft tap of stiletto heels as weight rolls to the ball of the foot.

Click, tap. Click, tap.

Keys shuffle and tinkle in the hand. She stifles them.

The ray shimmers through the sidelights and transom window and onto the walls.

Checkered shadows.

Dark house, but for the revolving beam.

She creeps by the parlor; her silhouette is large upon the wall.

She pauses, but why?

A peek and she sees the armchair by the fire.

The embers glow red.

The light beam wheels through the room; he has turned the chair around, she notices.

His scowl, raw. It freezes her.

The eyes glow red.

White lightning thunders through the dusky night.

A leaden thud; the crimson trickle on the spotless tile.

The acrid stench of gunpowder.

Bitter the taste of revenge, but sweet the satisfaction.

Black and white the room, red the dying fire.

Contemplation

Corey lies on his bed and contemplates the ceiling. His fixed gaze and his body's relaxed demeanor contrast against the racing thoughts in his mind. His life is at a crossroads, and his mind seeks to see as far ahead as possible in all directions before he chooses the path to follow. An innate risk-taker; Corey is always quick to realize and seize an opportunity. He knows the solution —the road to take at a crossroads—will always present itself.

Until now.

He has two choices: take the job out of state, or move back home and help his parents run the family business.

The job at the big corporation should be a straightforward decision, but still he doubts. It pays very well, and Corey is always open to new experiences. It is a job he has been striving for throughout his college years. He survived the grueling interview process and jumped with delight upon receiving the job offer. The company is solid and offers plenty of advancement opportunities. It even offers to help with MBA tuitions. Yet...

His other choice is to run the small shoe store his grandfather opened with blood, sweat and tears. It has survived against all odds, and chugged through The Great Depression, several economic downturns, and even the financial meltdown of the 21st-century, though with little expansion. It's profitable, and Corey would be the third generation to run it. Corey can see its future.

In his mind, he sees the 100th anniversary celebrations that will come in the next decade. In fact, he sees far beyond that. But there's no risk, no adventure in the meantime. The opportunity to expand is years away. And if he takes the corporate job, the adventure starts now.

So what's the problem? He thinks. Mom and Dad are still young and healthy, now is the time to try his hand at something else, and learn beyond what his grandfather and father learned in their lifetimes. Corey knows the shop will always be there, a haven to return to when his ship runs aground. So what stops him from taking the corporate job offer?

Corey sighs and shifts onto his side, facing the wall. His bedroom door clicks open, and he hears Dad's footsteps on the carpet. Confused, Corey turns to face him, but his heart stops when he sees his father's haggard and ashen face and his blue-tinged lips. Corey opens his mouth to speak, but no words come out. His father stands beside the bed, and gazes at him with the blank stare of a corpse. The apparition carries a gravestone. Shock snags Corey's breath when he notices the date.

At last, the words flow with the tears, "Will you be dead in two years?"

The apparition nods and fades into the dusky gloom seeping through the window. A sob strangles in Corey's throat; he reaches for the phone.

"Hello?" Dad's voice is a soothing balm.

"Dad," Corey chokes.

"Son! How are you? Did you get the job?"

"I'm fine, how are you?" Corey ignores the last question.

"Fine, fine. A little out of breath. Mom thinks I should see a doctor, but I'm sure it's nothing. The job?"

"No … I didn't get it," Corey lies.

In the end, the solution always appears.

Opportunity Knocks

Zoe leaned back in her chair and sighed. She gazed around the silent office and past the darkened cubicles surrounding hers. Down the aisle, she glimpsed the gloomy windows. She never enjoyed staying late, but the boss had heaped last-minute work on her and she thought it best to get it done as soon as possible. It didn't help matters she had spent the past half hour daydreaming about quitting the company.

It had taken her a while to admit it, but she did not like her job. She got along with everyone and always pasted an eternal smile on her lips. But, in the past few months, she had been dragging herself out of bed every weekday and resisting the urge to call in sick.

Things had been changing at the office; the new boss treated his employees like machines and had taken an especial dislike toward Zoe. Why? She could not say, but glancing around the empty office, it sure seemed true. He seemed to dump all eleventh-hour work on her, and only her.

Zoe rubbed her eyes and yawned. Exhausted, she glanced at her phone and saw a new text message from her friend, Norman. He had contacted her days ago and explained he was starting a business, wondering whether she would join him in the venture.

Zoe had said she needed time to consider it. In fact, she had been daydreaming about quitting this job and throwing all cares to the wind. She had been pondering Norman's offer.

"Zoe, I believe we'd be a helluva team," Norman's deep black eyes had fixed their serious gaze on her — one blue and one brown — heterochromatic eyes.

"But if I leave," Zoe rested her face in her hands, "I'll be taking a significant risk with my life. I also wouldn't have time to do both jobs. What should I do?"

Zoe contemplated her options for another moment before setting her hands on the keyboard. The characters on the screen melted into one giant blur; she blinked the exhaustion away and continued.

Muffled footsteps and the sound of shuffling papers distracted her. She glimpsed an older woman she did not know, walking toward the copier room. Zoe gazed after her; she thought she was the only person left in the building.

"Working late?" Zoe smiled as the woman returned to her own workstation.

The woman paused; an exhausted smile spread across her lips.

"Yes, I am. I wish I wasn't though, but there are bills to pay and I need the overtime."

"Yeah, I hear ya," Zoe said, "I need to get this done by tomorrow, some last-minute stuff my boss requested."

"Ah, yes, I worked for him many years ago."

"What was he like?" Zoe asked, eager for a break and a little gossip.

The woman leaned against Zoe's cubicle.

"Unkind and a terrible boss, somewhat of a bully, too. He enjoys demeaning and overworking the people he doesn't like. He tests the waters with them, and if they give an inch, he grabs a foot and then some. If I were you, I'd request a transfer. You're on his blacklist."

"How do you know?"

The woman shrugged, "You're the only one in his department working this late."

Zoe took a deep breath. As the woman turned to go, Zoe made a split-second decision.

"You know," she spoke and the woman, halting, attended her, "my friend has asked me to join him in a startup. I'm hesitant. I don't know what to do, it's like I'm between a rock and a hard place."

"What's keeping you from taking your friend's offer?"

Zoe thought for a moment, "Fear. I'm afraid it'll fail and I'll be out on my butt."

"What's the alternative?"

"Staying here, I suppose, and hoping a transfer goes through," Zoe shrugged, "maybe I'll search for another job, at another company as big and heartless as this one."

"I had an offer like that once. My friend Norm asked me to join him in a risky venture," The woman said in a voice brimming with melancholy and nostalgia.

Zoe caught her breath when she heard the name; she always called Norman 'Norm' because he never bent the rules.

"Wh-what happened?" Zoe stammered.

"I turned him down and stayed at my safe and cushy job, working under a boss who disrespected me at every turn. I applied for transfer after transfer to another department, but it was years before that came through. Found out later the boss had thwarted all my opportunities over and over until he couldn't anymore. By then, it was too late. Exhausted, I was drowning in debt with my small salary just keeping me afloat. Meanwhile, Norm and the person who took the offer I'd turned down were rolling in dough like Scrooge McDuck. In my darkest hour — unlike Scrooge McDuck — he loaned me some money, which went a long way."

She paused; Zoe gaped.

"I've always regretted turning down his job offer," she fixed her gaze on Zoe.

The woman stepped towards Zoe, who gasped when the light from the table lamp shone on the woman's eyes. One eye was blue, the other brown. Zoe's own face, drawn and haggard, stared back at her. The clock on the wall struck the hour and Zoe snapped her gaze away. When she turned back to the woman, no one was there.

Savasana

Alice laid down in Savasana and shut her eyes. She let the music flow over her as her muscles relaxed. She could almost feel the notes as they meandered through the calm of the Yoga studio; her sanctuary. Meditation was her haven and Yoga, her release. These were the few moments she allowed herself to be with herself and let all else disappear. Let the world turn, she always thought when practice began.

Throughout class, Alice sensed she was about to remember something. Breathing through the poses as her mind drifted away from the day-to-day, from James and her situation, and focusing on the moment, the movement, the breathing, she had the strange sensation that she had forgotten something, or rather that something she had forgotten was about to come to light. Like this thing, or feeling, was trying to push itself forward into the forefront of her mind. And now, during final relaxation, she let her muscles melt into the mat, her chest opened to the ceiling and her arms and legs stretched out before her.

I ask for enlightenment and guidance, Alice thought, inhaling and relishing in the warm air that filled her lungs. She wished for a glimpse into the future as she exhaled. The instructor dimmed the lights.

Darkness filled her mind, and she let it carry her away. Alice noted the music fading—perhaps the instructor had lowered the volume — and breathed as she pushed the thought away, letting it linger only for a moment before it dissipated into the vastness of her mind. Thoughts came and went like soft blossoms blowing in the wind, drifting and hovering, or wavering far beyond her reach. Each breath took her farther away from the outside world and deeper inside her mind. She was now at the threshold between wakefulness and sleep, though her body was still present —she could hear and smell and feel—yet noise and scent were like her thoughts now, a passing sensation only to be acknowledged and blown away.

The soft padding of the instructor's bare feet vibrated as he walked by Alice's mat. Alice sensed the footfalls belonged to someone else, and tried to open her eyes, but they remained closed under eyelids heavy like a thick membrane. She perceived she was somewhere else, and in her mind's eye, she saw a battlefield. Wet grass seeped its coldness into her bones and the smell of blood pierced her nostrils with its sharp iron scent. Bodies scattered all around her and as she tried to move her arms, she was certain the right one was gone; the pain of its absence filling her heart with anguish and helplessness. People walked around, she felt their heavy footfalls, no longer the soft bare feet of the instructor but pounding leather steps that shook the damp ground where she lay.

Alice tried to pull herself out of this vivid nightmare, but it held her fast. She was scared and cold and as she tried to move, to get up, to wake up, she felt nothing but sharp rending pain that sent bolts of lightning through her mangled body. The terrifying realization that she was on that battlefield only heightened her fear and strengthened the hold this new reality had on her. The Yoga studio, with its giant mirrors and wooden floor was gone. So was the soft lighting and the relaxing music. Instead, there was blood-soaked grass and the smell of leather, metal and death. And the pain.

Alice felt someone leaning over her, the pungent stench of his sweat penetrating her open mouth as her breathing came in hard severed gasps. Breathe, she kept telling herself, deep breath in, deep breath out. But a watery wall in her chest hampered the incoming air, and as it blew out of her, she wanted to reach out and grab it. She wanted to eat it, to put it in her mouth and stop it with the palms of her hands until it fought its way down to her lungs.

"This one won't live," he said to someone who stood beside her.

She knew the words and their meaning, but they were not in English. The language sounded ancient, and it reminded her of sunlight winding down the streets of Rome and of the rainbow over Vesuvius in Pompeii. But this new language lacked the singsong appeal of the warm Mediterranean and the words seemed shorter and staccato. Yet, she knew she spoke this language. This was the language of this new armless life and this new airless world.

The man kneeled down beside her and the warmth of his body invaded the surrounding space, hovering like dense jelly and only just beyond her reach. Alice envied this man who breathed with air flowing into and nurturing the warm blood that ran its course down his body uninterrupted by sundered limbs. She tried to open her eyes to let them know she was conscious, but all she could muster was a faint moan. Then a strange rattling sound erupted from her throat as she felt her lungs collapse and the ocean inside them spill into her mouth and out of her parted lips. It tasted like blood. Her chest seemed to crumble in an instant and she no longer felt the thump of her heart resonating in the wet ground. This is Death; this last thought pushed itself forward in her frightened yet addled mind as she plunged into the final darkness. She laid there, just another corpse on the battlefield.

Then music filled her ears and her space again. Soft at first, it grew louder and stronger until it coursed down her head, her neck, her chest and filled her limbs. The instructor's voice sounded warm and clear, golden even, like the break of a new day.

"Let's come out of Corpse Pose by moving our fingers and our toes, then our arms and legs and taking a big stretch."

Alice begged her body to wiggle the fingers of her right hand, and they responded. Her heart lit up as an imaginary weight lifted off her chest. She took a deep breath and imagined her lungs filling up like the big red balloons she loved as a child. As she let go of the air inside her, she stroked the soft wood of the floor beneath her fingers and bent her elbows. She wiggled her toes and bent her knees. Alice rested her hands on her belly and smiled, emanating relief from every pore. She rolled onto her right side and she pressed her forehead down on the mat; she gave thanks for this life and this body. She sat up cross-legged and with a final Ohm the practice ended. As she rolled up her mat, the tears threatened to burst out, but she swallowed them. She was trembling from joy and fear and gratitude, but wanted no one to notice. How would I explain this? She thought as people walked around her.

Alice stood up and caught the movement reflected in the mirror with the corner of her eye. She turned and expected to see her own tall, slim figure, with black Yoga pants, purple tank top, and her blond hair in its customary ponytail. Instead, she saw The Soldier. He was short, dark and muscular, with strong square features and eyes ablaze with thunder and courage. The image startled her, and she stepped back. The Soldier did the same. Alice looked around her; everyone had already left. The studio was bathed in the blue light of dusk and the last rays of the setting sun shone an amber path down the maple-wood floor to where she stood. She cradled her right arm and almost burst into tears when The Soldier copied the movement. He wore full Roman armor, with sword—Gladius—at his side.

Alice and The Soldier stepped towards the mirror. They were face to face now, her soft features reflecting his sharp ones. She looked into his intense eyes and saw her own timid gaze peeking out from the storm raging inside his dark pupils. They raised their right arms and touched the mirror, her fingertips mirroring his. In that instant, Alice knew everything about The Soldier's life and understood it had once been her own. She had wished for a glimpse into the future and had seen the past instead.

At last, that memory that had been trying to escape oblivion exploded in her mind and she saw a humble birth and a tough childhood. She closed her eyes and rested her forehead on the mirror. Alice remembered everything: the hardship, the poverty, the wars. But also remembered the courage. In The Soldier's body, she had once been valiant, strong and determined. No risk was too frightening, no feat too dangerous. She had always been first on the battlefield and fought the hardest. She had lived by the sword and had died by it. She had been transported to this death during the meditation and now understood she needed to recall this past life to move on with the present one. The memory of the last moments of The Soldier's life vanquished the fear and despair of her situation, and she now found the enlightenment and guidance she sought.

She was at a crossroads: she had to choose between giving life or halting it; and now knew what she must do. Alice placed her hands on her belly and gazed at it. The tears broke through her eyes and streamed down her face. She chose life.

"My little one, I have nothing to give you now but my love and your name: Vitus. It was my name once, and it gave me courage in another life. It's bright and powerful, and I know you'll wear it well."

The sound of her voice broke through the darkening studio and vibrated against the cool glass of the mirror.

Alice looked up, and The Soldier was gone, leaving her own reflection in his place. She looked into her soft blue eyes and saw only the person she had seen all her life: meek, mild, and scared. At least, this was the person James had taught her to see. But not anymore, she thought, and a radiant glimpse of The Soldier shimmered in her reflected pupils.

Alice picked up her mat, put on her shoes, and walked out of the studio. She drove home, packed a suitcase, and left James a final note.

"It'll be just you and me now, little Vitus. No more fear, no more hesitation, no more abuse. We'll always stand tall, even if the world crumbles around us."

The Old Manor

Rhonda slammed on the brakes; the tiny Kia skidded to a stop. She peeked out from the passenger-side window, mouth agape and head weaving this way and that to get a better look. Every day she drove past this spot and she knew the corner where she'd stopped had, until yesterday, been a vacant lot.

It had been so for years. She recalled vague memories of sirens and running feet in the night when the Old Manor had burned to the ground. She must have been, what, five, six years old? It had been an enormous tragedy, and in it, the family had died out. Ever since that space had remained empty, weeds had overgrown the remnants of the foundations until it looked like any vacant lot.

Now, the Old Manor stood in splendor, just as she'd seen in her grandfather's pictures. He'd been an avid photographer and had chronicled the Old Manor since its heyday until its blazing demise. The house was a mishmash of different architectural styles, built upon by several generations, complete with turrets, a wide verandah and a widow's walk.

Rhonda climbed out of her car and gazed around the deserted street. With no one around, the house appeared unnoticed. Crickets and cicadas chirped and buzzed in the trees; the scorching sun beat down on her stinging shoulders. Drenched in sweat, her tank top stuck to her body.

She tiptoed into the gated yard, fenced in by tall wrought-iron bars, polished and new, unlike the rusty remnants she'd seen all her life. Glancing every which way, she stepped to the door and searched the wall for a doorbell. She found none and knocked, pressing her ears to the door. She thought she heard footsteps within and a murmur of voices. Rhonda frowned and peeked in the first window on the wide verandah. She gasped.

Rhonda ran back to the door and tried the knob. It opened and, heart beating, she entered. The lavish interior reminded Rhonda of her visit to the Gilded Age mansions in Newport, Rhode Island. Yet, unlike those museums, this house felt alive, not a hodgepodge of old-fashioned furniture on display.

She ventured further into the house, following the sounds of voices and music, until she came upon a party.

"What's happening?" Rhonda murmured, "Is this a play? Are they filming a movie?"

Ladies dressed in lacy high collars, long dresses and elbow gloves danced on the arms of handsome men in three-piece suits and copious mustaches; pearls and feathered fans everywhere. A quartet played a lively waltz.

"Pardon me, madam," someone spoke at her shoulder. Rhonda turned. A man in butler's garb and white gloves offered her a drink from a silver tray. Rhonda, always shy and awkward, shook her head and ran back to her Kia.

She sped past the houses she knew so well, screeched to a stop at her house, and, calling for her husband Bert, ran up the drive-way.

"The house," she panted. She pointed and tugged at his sleeved, unable to explain in words what she had experienced.

Bert, mild-mannered and easy-going, tried calming her, but she grabbed him by the lapel and shoved him into the car. The Kia lurched and screeched as she turned around and zoomed past neighbors walking their dogs without a wave of acknowledgment.

Rhonda slammed on the brakes; the Kia skidded to a stop.

"What is it?" Bert asked, alarmed.

Rhonda stared openmouthed at the vacant lot where the Old Manor had burned down long ago.

A Life in a Letter

My dearest Christine,

Reading this will seem like a voice coming to you from the grave. By the time you find this letter, I will have been dead forty-two years. You need to know I have been with you your whole life and I saw it mapped out the day I found out you were coming into this world. I cried in my dingy apartment, wondering how I would make it with a fatherless child and living on minimum-wage when there you were, a picture so clear I could almost touch it. I saw you taking your first steps toward me, wearing the same purple dress my mother had bought for me. Later, you sat in my lap as you read "Peter Pan" to me for the first time. I was so proud I cried. Then you came home, braces in your teeth, brandishing the medal you won at your school's in-house dance competition.

Years later, I was cheering for you at the Royal Albert Hall as you were crowned International Ballroom Dancing Champion, with Jack standing next to you so tall and proud. That was also the night you told me you were pregnant.

I wept when I first met my grandson, because I also saw his life before me and I knew he wouldn't be here long. So I urged you to stop dancing and spend more time with him. I don't care that you kicked me out. I don't care that we didn't talk for a decade. I don't care that I never saw my grandson in life again; I had let him go the moment I met him. I knew I would have all eternity with him. I waited for your call on that horrible day. You never knew this, but my purse already hung on my arm when I picked up the phone.

Perhaps now you're wondering why I never told you of his death beforehand, or of Jack's leaving, but you must understand, had you known or not, nothing would have changed. Tommy was supposed to die when he did and you cannot control Jack's decisions. I'm so proud that you never let these events weaken your spirit. I saw in reality, not in my mind's eye, how much stronger and brighter you became.

I know it was difficult to accept that living alone at seventy was no longer possible. I know you think you gave up your past when you packed up your house and moved into the nursing home. They gave you the same room I had twenty years ago. I left this life in that room and tonight, after sixteen years, you will leave it, too. Don't be afraid, my daughter; Tommy and I are here. Peter Pan was right, Death is the biggest adventure of all. Close your eyes now and we will be together. Forever.

My Unconditional Love to you,

Mom

The Snake

Muriel gazed at herself in the mirror and searched for the young girl she had seen all her life, but found only the baggy-eyed crone she had become. She breathed a shaky sigh as tears threatened to well up and burst like geysers out of her already red and puffy eyes.

"Ugly," The Snake whispered.

She knew The Snake well; it lived inside her and told her harsh truths. Relentless and cruel, it slithered around her synapses in a slow meander that never stopped.

Muriel wondered when The Snake had wormed itself into her mind.

"I was never like this," she whispered, afraid to speak up lest The Snake hissed again.

Muriel closed her eyes and pictured Mom, the one genuine memory she had of her: a hug, given when she was just a child. Although Muriel sometimes thought it might be only a dream.

When The Snake first took up residence in her mind, the memory of Muriel's long-dead mother was strong enough to clamp down on it and silence its forked tongue. But now, Mom's memory was often powerless against the petty, demeaning words The Snake whispered.

"Ugly," The Snake said again, "he'll leave you because you're ugly."

And the tears welled up and spilled over Muriel's closed eyelids, wetting her eyelashes so they clumped together into a salty mess.

"He won't," Muriel challenged The Snake, but deep inside she knew it only spoke the truth.

He no longer cared. He no longer loved her. She did nothing right; she was such a klutz, such a weirdo. The Snake was on a roll, and its venomous words slithered all over Muriel's mind until it filled with the poison-green thoughts of despair and worthlessness. It also defiled Mom's memory; Muriel tried to cling to it as it burned away like an old film on fire.

"Stop it!" She cried and opened her eyes.

The bathroom was green, and Muriel, for an instant, believed the toxin had oozed out of her and tainted the bathroom, her sanctuary. The last place where she could be herself, where she could cheer herself, and enjoy the peace and warmth of a cleansing bath. Here she could leave her body and her mind and hold on to Mom's memory, just as long as she never looked in the mirror.

Tonight, Muriel had dawdled too long, and the steam had peeled itself off the glass before she finished dressing and was ready to leave her sanctuary. It had taken one glance, and now the bathroom glowed toxic green.

Muriel rubbed her eyes and opened them again. The green veil dissipated, and as her eyes adjusted, she spotted a blurry figure in the mirror gazing back at her.

"Ugly," The Snake jeered again as the image in the glass sharpened.

"Why are you here?" Muriel asked The Snake, "Where did you come from?"

"You need me," The Snake replied, "you made me."

"Lie!" The reflection in the mirror screamed and startled Muriel, who placed her hand across her mouth, astonished by what she beheld.

The reflection glared back with Muriel's girlish face and fiery eyes—the image she searched for every time she dared peek in the mirror. Now here she was, that young, graceful girl with bouncy curls and bright eyes, scowling at her. Her eyes blazed with fury, and Muriel was thunderstruck that the image she sought for so long would glare back at her in wrath; the past angry at the present.

"He brought The Snake," The Reflection fixed its scorching gaze on Muriel, "he planted it in your brain with his boorishness and his belittling comments and deeds."

As Muriel stared into those seething pupils, realization broke through the toxic green fog in her mind, and the same spark of ire that burned in The Reflection's eyes kindled in Muriel's chest and rose to her cheeks, then flowed down to her toes until her whole body, her whole self was ablaze with wrath and indignation.

The Reflection raised its hand, though Muriel stood motionless, transfixed, as all his actions, comments and jokes replayed in her mind. It reached its arm out towards Muriel and broke through the smooth barrier of the glass as its fingers neared Muriel's forehead.

The Snake hissed and bared its hideous poison-filled fangs. It lunged towards The Reflection, but The Reflection grabbed it, ripped it out of Muriel's brain and dashed it against the medicine cabinet. The door sprang open, and the contents spilled onto the vanity. Muriel gazed at the mess with stunned eyes. All the little instruments and lotions she used to make herself presentable to him, to please him, lay scattered on the white granite countertop.

A disgusted sneer crept up Muriel's lips, and a low growl escaped her throat.

She flung open the bathroom door. The steamy poison, neutralized by the anger-fire that flared inside her, seeped into the hall. Muriel paid it no mind. She put on her shoes, grabbed her purse, and walked out the front door.

All she took from that house was Mom's memory, now shining brighter than ever.

Ripper

Dainty heels click-clack on the pavement and approach the dark alley. He hides in a doorway, the dim gaslight of the streetlamp shines only on the blade peeking out from his sleeve. His features are in shadow, yet, in the darkness, he smirks.

The heels approach, and the woman rounds the corner, entering the alley. The sputtering gas-lamp flickers as she walks by, but he sees the seductive radiance emanating from her. She shines with the light of the brightest star.

Does she not know a murderer lurks the streets?

He wants her.

He chooses her.

He waits as she passes by the gloomy doorway, oblivious to his shadowy presence. He slithers in the gloom, his footfalls soundless on the cobblestone. Her footsteps echo in the night.

The fingers clasping the cold dagger twitch, and his nostrils flare, anticipating the aroma of flowing blood. It is a metallic perfume so powerful in its seductiveness, he must bathe in it again and again.

She walks on and nears the next gaslight.

He reaches out and grabs her.

She snarls.

The blade flashes in the dim light.

The street is abuzz with the rumor the killer has struck again. Police shove their way through the crowd huddled in the alleyway. In the soft light of dawn, they expect the sight of a woman's torn corpse.

They find a man instead; a dagger lies beside him.

Jagged fang marks slash his throat, and his eyes stare, frozen in abject terror.

It's the Guys from "Supernatural"

The highway stretched into the distance; the cold jagged peaks in the horizon never neared.

Karla and Rachel sat in congenial silence while Bruno Mars played on the stereo. Half of the long drive was already behind them. The full moon rose in the shimmering sky as the sun set at their back.

"Huh," Rachel breathed, "seems like we're going backwards."

"What do you mean?"

"Yeah, we're driving towards the darkness as we leave the light behind us. Like moving away from life, towards death."

Karla sniggered, "Don't be such a Debbie Downer."

Rachel chuckled.

The long drive was only the start of a long goodbye and yes, Karla was aware they drove towards death. The ultimate destination of Grandpa's long life.

Karla glanced in the rearview mirror. A black classic car was tailgating them, pushing them to drive faster.

"Look, it's the guys from *Supernatural*," Karla said as the car changed into the fast lane.

The sisters watched it overtake them.

It was a Chevy Impala, but an earlier model and a convertible, unlike the one featured in the show. The top was down and two impatient women laughed and whooped into Karla's side mirror.

The driver wore a baby-blue headscarf wrapped around her hair, which billowed behind her; one gloved hand on the wheel, the other draped over the door. The passenger had a ponytail tied with a pink ribbon and curled into a single ringlet; she wore red Lolita heart-shaped sunglasses. The Impala's bat-wing fins zipped by and the cat-eye taillights squinted at them as the car heaved and revved, then sped into the horizon.

"Grandpa would have loved that," Rachel grinned, "it was a 50s model, right?"

"Yep, he would know the exact year and the whole shebang, too. He talks a blue streak about cars."

Rachel giggled.

The drive continued; blue shadows fell over the landscape.

Karla and Rachel would stop at a motel. As Rachel read out the upcoming exits, Karla glanced in the rearview mirror.

"Huh," she said, "the guys from *Supernatural* behind us again."

The sisters fell silent as the eager black car overtook them and the women zoomed past with reckless abandon.

"Gosh, Karly, that was the same car!"

"I know, right! But how? At what point did we pass them?"

"Maybe they stopped for a bite somewhere?"

"Maybe."

Karla doubted but stayed silent; she didn't recall any rest stops…

The road stretched ahead; they would soon be near their stopover. As they approached their exit, a car pulled up behind them. It drew close and honked.

"I think it's the same car again," Karla frowned at the rearview mirror.

Rachel glanced back, "No way…"

"Ooh, that's our exit," she exclaimed as they passed a road sign.

Karla slowed down and signaled. The black car followed close in rude impatience. They took the offramp; the Impala pushing them to go faster. Karla resisted because she knew not how dangerous the junction into the state highway would be. The Chevy sped up as they rounded a curve and overtook them. Both women glared at the sisters as they passed; the pony-tailed passenger—her heart-shaped sunglasses now atop her head—stuck her tongue out at them.

The black car squeezed in front of Karla's Honda and merged onto the state highway.

Karla screamed and slammed on the brakes when it disappeared under the nose of a semi-trailer truck with a horrible crunch and a flash of metal. Karla's own car skidded with screeching brakes; Rachel shrieked. Karla maneuvered onto the shoulder; they came to a trembling stop. The truck zoomed past, not stopping for the black wreck in the grassland.

Rachel jumped out and ran towards the wreckage as Karla's shaking fingers fumbled for her phone. She was about to dial 911 when Rachel's perplexed expression in the beams of the headlight stopped her. She ran out to meet her sister.

"What the…?"

"There's no one here," Rachel choked, "there's no one!"

Karla stared. Rachel was right, there was no one. The metal remains were rusty and overgrown with grass and devoid of humans.

A cloud covered the moon and darkened the landscape. Rachel felt for Karla's hand; the car-wreck disappeared! Nothing remained on the arid grass by the highway. As the moon shone again, something glinted in the grass at Rachel's feet. She picked up the rusty 1950s Chevrolet hood emblem encrusted in the bent rims of heart-shaped sunglasses.

Ella

Ella sat by the window; moonlight cast a silvery glow over the snow-covered ground and the smooth surface of the frozen lake. Stars scintillated in the heavens, and Ella marveled at how bright they seemed despite the moon's radiant glow. The wind crooned through the window and picked up stray flurries that glittered like fluttering grains of sugar. Frost settled over the snow and froze the powdery fluff so that moonbeams caught the individual crystals here and there, sparkling like diamonds on the soft ground; a mirror image of the twinkling stars in the sky. An owl hooted nearby, and the sound seemed to cast a spell over the shimmering landscape.

There must be magic tonight, Ella thought, good magic, as the world seems sprinkled with sugar, like icing on a cake.

Ella pulled her cream-colored flannel robe over her paisley blue pajamas and turned away from the window. She glanced at her bed with its purple flowered bedspread and the one teddy bear she had not yet parted with leaning against the pillow. Over the last few months, she had exchanged her toys for posters of cute boy bands and celebrities. Necklaces and bracelets now dangled from the corners of her vanity's mirror, and a jewelry box had replaced the Barbie dolls sitting atop the dresser.

She reached into the pocket of her robe, and, smiling, took out her very first brand-new lipstick. She had cajoled her mother into buying it for her. The color was a soft pink hue, though she had tried to convince her mother the bright red "Cadillac Heart" shade suited her better.

"No baloney, Miss Mahoney," her mother had put her foot down and glared.

Beside the jewelry box stood the bottle of her first perfume, which her beloved aunt gave her as a birthday gift. It had started the transformation inside her.

Facing the mirror, Ella traced the lipstick over her lips, marveling at how the paint changed their appearance. She pressed her lips together to even out the color—like her aunt taught her — then puckered them and beamed at herself, giggling.

Ella sighed and returned her gaze to the sugary cake-world outside her window. A glimmer in the sky caught her eye, and the thought she should wish upon that star flashed, but her new grown-up mind stifled that spark.

"You're too old to believe in fairytales," she chided herself; the owl hooted once, as if disagreeing.

The star, one of many, flickered again and, unbidden, the wish for a handsome prince blossomed in her mind. Feeling silly, Ella slid her feet off the window-seat.

She was turning away when she caught movement out of the corner of her eye. She fixed her gaze on the frozen lake. Her heart pounded as a figure floated across the ice. In the moonlight, she discerned someone approaching her house.

She gulped; was it possible her wish was coming true? She wondered whether to call her parents, who were watching TV in the living room; the muffled sound of the program seeped through the otherwise silent home. Yet something kept her rooted to the spot. Awe, perhaps, mingled with a tad of apprehension.

The figure neared and crossed the property boundary into the backyard. Ella grinned; the moonlight shone on the figure of a young man about her age. He was handsome, like the boy celebrities plastered on her wall. He glided with a cool swagger and, as he reached her window, a smile lit up his face.

Ella and the shimmering prince gazed at one another through the frost-lined pane. The prince reached out his hand and placed it on the glass, beaming his royal smile.

"Let me in," his mellifluous voice broke the frozen silence, "I'm cold."

Ella contemplated his beautiful eyes as her hand edged towards the latch. Her fingers closed around it.

She blushed at the boy's adoring gaze, while her brain instructed her wrist to turn the latch and open the window.

An instant later, Ella gasped and yanked her hand back, shaking her head. She had caught the flash of malice in the prince's eyes. Her heart thundered in her ears and chills crawled up her spine.

The prince scowled, and his whole countenance darkened.

"Let me in," he demanded, but Ella shook her head.

She opened her mouth to scream, but terror caught in her throat as the glass splintered where the prince's fingers still rested upon it.

"Let me in," he growled, but Ella refused.

Help me, she thought, her mind racing as she noticed the fiery-red glare of the prince's pupils. They burned into her like hot, furious coals.

"Let me in," he snarled and gnashed his teeth.

"No," she whimpered.

Someone help me, please, she implored.

The prince-demon balled his talon-fingers into a fist. Ella felt her heart would burst out of her chest. The prince-demon drew back the fist and was about to smash the window, when a Snowy Owl swooped down upon him. Amid the flutter of blinding white and bloodcurdling screeches, Ella shrieked as the prince-demon shattered into a thousand glowing cinders that dissipated into the night.

The Light

Why? Why? Why? Why was no one moving?

The light had been green for thirty seconds, and the five cars in front of Joey did not budge. All Joey wanted was to get home, heat a TV dinner, watch sitcoms and leave the rough workday behind him. The boss had been mean and stressed out, and one thing after another had gone wrong, like quicksand.

"Freedom!" he had said as he raced out of the office building.

Now he wished he could take it back. Maybe it had been that call for freedom that triggered the traffic jam. Sitting in his car for almost two hours, Joey felt like the entire universe was conspiring to boycott his evening. Everything on the street: the stalled cars, the unsynchronized traffic lights, the abnormal amount of trucks and buses were all punishing him for having dared to think the helluva day was over and done.

"This is Murphy's Law," he mumbled, "Just when you think things can't get worse, they do."

At last, the cars began to move. He took his foot off the brake and rolled forward.

"Son of a bitch!" he exclaimed when the traffic light turned yellow, then red.

With one eye on the traffic light, and the other on the cars crossing the intersection, Joey's impatience increased. The cars were zooming past him, and the road ahead lay empty, not a car in sight, including the five that had made it through the earlier green light. It seemed the street was mocking him, sticking its tongue out at him and chanting, "you can't move! You can't move! I'm free and you can't move!"

He waited for the light to turn green, but it just wouldn't.

A blue Volkswagen Sedan drove by with a million people in it. An ambulance followed right after, its siren screaming as it tried to pass the blue Sedan that was so old and riding so low it could not move out of the way fast enough. Then a few more cars passed, and still the light did not turn green.

How much longer is this gonna last? He thought as a green minivan with a team of shrieking little leaguers and a happy beagle sticking its head and tongue out the window crossed the intersection. Joey glanced at his watch and figured he had been at the stop light for over three minutes, and still the cars kept cruising in front of him.

A frenetic honking; a red convertible sports car tried to overtake a bus, which was going so slow it seemed stationary.

"I know how you feel," murmured Joey, as the pair drove away.

The stop light; red.

Maybe the stop light broke at that last change, and he should try to cross with caution. He glanced at the other drivers beside him, but they seemed unpreoccupied that the light had been stuck on red forever.

He gazed ahead, just in time to see the blue Volkswagen Sedan go by again. It couldn't be the same one, no way. But then the ambulance wailed, and it tried to pass the Sedan once more.

Joey glanced at the light; still red.

The hands on his watch had not moved at all. Is it broken? He thought, maybe the batteries are dead. He tapped and shook the watch by his ear, listening for its ticking.

Dead.

Joey sighed and saw the green minivan pass. What were the chances of two minivans with screaming kids and a beagle crossing the same intersection just minutes apart? Zero.

Joey stared at the red light, scratching his head. Was it a hallucination? Déjà vu?

The frenetic honking blared through his confusion, and he saw the sports car trying to pass the slow bus once more. He turned to the drivers beside him and a chill ran up his spine. The other drivers gazed straight ahead, as if out on a Sunday drive, with no worry and no hurry.

And still the light stayed red.

Joey's impatience simmered into anguish, and his anguish boiled into fear as the Volkswagen crept by a third time, followed by the wailing ambulance, the minivan and the sports car.

Joey breathed with quick and shallow gasps, and his pulse began to race. Now, he didn't care about the beer or the TV dinner. Was he stuck in time? Was he ever going to move? Was he doomed to sit there forever, always expecting the light to turn green?

He closed his eyes and took deep breaths as the ambulance approached yet again, while the blue Sedan inched to get out of the way. Then he heard the noisy kids in the minivan and knew the honking sports car would follow.

Honk! honk! honk!

Joey opened his eyes as the convertible tried to zig-zag around the bus. He closed his eyes again and listened for the ambulance, the kids and the sports car, wishing the nightmare would end as the minivan shrieked by him.

He tried to relax; the convertible announced its coming. Honk! Honk! Honk! and it would be gone, only to drive by the next time around, forever.

This time, the honking didn't stop. Joey opened his eyes and heard the commotion behind him.

The light; green.

Everyone was honking at him to move. Joey hit the accelerator so hard the car lurched forward as it shifted gears, and in one second, Joey crossed the intersection and was cruising down the road with no other cars in sight.

Ghost Memories

Dusk glimmers on the bench as the wind sweeps the ghostly shadows of a long-forgotten summer. I remember two children sitting on that bench, their futures lying ahead of them as vast as the lake before them, which always seemed as open and magnificent as the sea.

The summer of wonder and revelations ended with the tumultuous whirlpool of surprise and powerful undertow that carried me away. Yet, standing here now, the memories flow out of me like the cleansing light of the setting sun. How I wish to go back to that time, to that age when everything was simple, black or white, dead or alive, day or night. Even dawn and dusk seemed opposites; not transitions, not limbo.

I look around and see the change. How long have I been here? How many years? Ages? Eons? I stayed, wanting to stop time, and in return I have only forgotten.

Walpurgis Night

Jenna sat by the window of her new, old bedroom in her grandmother's house. Two fat tears hovered on her eyelids, then rolled down her cheeks. Her parents had moved into the house soon after she died, and those tears were not just over Oma's death (her presence still lingered over the house), but also over the big change that came with the big move.

Jenna missed the many friends she left behind in her old town and regretted her status as the new girl. She had not yet found her footing and her place at her new school.

"Kids are meaner here," she told Mom, "they pull away as soon as they find out I'm related to Oma. It's not like Hexer is a common name around here, I can't deny my relation."

Mom sighed, "I'm sorry, honey, but we had to move after the company downsized and let Dad go."

"I know, Mom," Jenna replied, and curled her lip over her braces, a gesture now so common Mom wondered if it would stay after the braces came off Jenna's teeth.

"But why do they hate Oma? They say she's a jinx."

"Because she was German, and lonely, and never spoke English well, so people never understood her. They saw a war bride, someone who used your grandpa as a ticket out of poverty and misery. To them, she was an enchantress who charmed her way into his life and his money."

"But that's not true," Jenna exclaimed, "they loved one another, didn't they?"

"Oh yes, they loved each other very much," Mom answered, "but people only see what they want to see. We know she was loving and kind, but no one here gave her a chance."

A lump lodged in Jenna's throat, "I miss her. I miss her stories."

"Stories?"

"Sure, she used to tell me stories all the time."

Dad spoke German to Jenna, and it facilitated the relationship between Jenna and Oma. It made Mom grateful to know Jenna had been emotionally close—if not physically—to her only grandmother, having grown up never knowing her own grandparents herself.

"What stories did she tell you?"

"She loved to talk about her childhood, her town, and her family. She spoke about the big family gatherings, and the dance halls," Jenna's eyes sparkled, then darkened a little when she continued, "although these last few years, she would tell me about witches convening on Walpurgisnacht. She said she saw them through her window, dancing in the moonlight."

Mom pursed her lips at Jenna's last remark, "Remember, Oma had senile dementia for a long time, so you should take her stories with a grain of salt."

Jenna smiled and nodded, and returned to her room to sit by the window and watch the night fall over the meadow behind the house. She opened the window and let the spring breeze waft through the room. The stars winked at her as they appeared one by one, and the moon rose above the treetops, casting its cool glow over the meadow as it bid farewell to April with full pomp and circumstance.

"Why are you crying?" Oma's voice floated through Jenna's mind.

"Because I miss you, Omi," Jenna said, and the wind rustled through the trees.

"I am here," Oma's whisper swept through the meadow, borne on the wind puffing through the tall grass.

Whirlwinds of leaves blew across the silvery moonlight. Mist descended from the mountain and billowed through the forest and into the meadow like long and slender will-o'-the-wisps twirling and swaying to the melody of the gusting, fragrant wind.

The moonlight caught the mist-tendrils and shone on them with an eerie, yet playful, glow. They might have been graceful girls dancing naked in the moonlight.

Jenna smiled; Oma's witches on Walpurgisnacht.

Jem Thompson

Jem Thompson's childhood best friend was Bruise, a mongrel dog mixed with stray, with a gray-black patch over his eye. Bruise died when Jem was a teen, and he missed his friend so much he never kept another pet again. There could be no other like Bruise.

Marriage, kids, grandkids, widowerhood.

Every day, Jem Thompson would walk in the park that faced his house and sit on the bench by the mermaid fountain at its eastern corner. There he would watch the comings and goings of his neighbors, and revel in the games they played with their dogs.

Late in the afternoon on a cloudy day, Jem Thompson sat at his bench longer than usual; fluffy white clouds had kept the beaming sun at bay and a cool breeze blew. He laid his head back on the hard wooden seat and took a brief nap. A cold wetness surprised Jem Thompson, and he awoke to find Bruise's soulful eyes gazing at him as the dog licked Jem's fingers.

"Bruise?" Jem Thompson muttered in disbelief.

The dog yipped and Jem Thompson recognized Bruise, not another dog that looked like him. Bruise nuzzled his hand and then nudged Jem Thompson, now an old man, to follow him. The dog was relentless, and, with a snap of bones and a creak of the old knee, Jem Thompson stood, his hip jutting out sideways. Bruise walked a few paces, then returned to coax his old friend.

With his slow and crooked gait, Jem Thompson followed his long-gone dog. It never occurred to him to fear the animal; this was Bruise, after all.

Bruise led him across the street and down a narrow alley, away from the square with the park at its center he had known so well for forty-odd years. He walked past houses he had not seen in decades. Not since Madge's death, and the creaky knee had forced him into an almost sedentary life. He came to a brick-red townhouse that stood between two modern bungalows. Jem Thompson recalled it had been part of a row of townhouses; now it was the last one standing. The plain, modern eyesores had replaced the others.

Jem sighed, winded and tired; Bruise trotted to the door. He barked and scratched it. The sun was low in the sky and Jem, unaware of how far he had walked, stood like a fool before the house.

Bruise returned to his side and snapped at Jem's hand, the way he had always done when he had wanted something from him. Jem sighed, and, shaking his head, tottered up the front path. He stood at the door, uneasy. With a deep breath, he rang the bell. An old woman opened. They stared at one another for a moment, then Jem's eyes went from dull to shining with recognition.

"Fanny?" He said, surprised, "Fanny Markowitz?"

A slow smile spread over the woman's face, "Jem Thompson, well I'll be damned! It's been, what, sixty years?"

Jem smiled at his old friend and was about to reply when a loud bang rattled the house.

"What the…?" Fanny exclaimed and turned to enter when Jem pulled her back.

"I smell gas!" he yelled.

He took Fanny's withered hand and led her to the street. Tongues of fire licked the kitchen curtains. Smoke billowed from the upstairs window-frames and, in the next instant, flames erupted from the shattered glass.

"Serena!" Fanny yelled.

"Is someone else inside the house?" Jem asked in alarm.

"Serena, my cat!" Fanny screamed, "I need to get her!"

She was about to lunge into the flames when they distinguished the silhouette of a dog in the gaping doorway. It carried something in its muzzle.

Away from the burning house, the dog set the dangling bundle on the ground; it jerked and moved and ran to Fanny. Fanny cradled the calico cat in her arms. Jem turned to pet the dog, but Bruise had disappeared.

Fanny whispered beside him, "That was Bruise, wasn't it?"

Jem nodded and moved his lips, but wailing sirens drowned out his answer.

Mirrors and Smoke

"If it's too good to be true," Grandpa had often said, "leave it. There's always a catch."

Nothing in Damon's life had ever been too good to be true, and he often wondered whether that philosophy had inflicted missed opportunities upon his family. Yet, here was the job offer.

Damon's heart beat with delight as he read the letter. The company offered extraordinary benefits, and the salary, oh, the salary, those zeroes went through the roof. He gulped; in one month, he stood to earn more money than his parents had earned in their lifetime of toil and trouble and backbreaking overtime at the factory.

"It's honest work, Damon," his father's words whispered in his memory, "never forget that. We are decent people, and that's far more rewarding than money."

It annoyed Damon that now, in his moment of victory, when he should savor pure bliss, those words would haunt him and a nagging apprehension would settle in his heart. He had struggled too; being the first in his family with a college degree had been no picnic. And he worked his fingers to the bone at his meager-paying entry-level job while he clung for dear life to the bottom rung of the corporate ladder.

Then, that phone call. A headhunter saw his profile. A company, unknown but successful, was interested in his credentials.

Afterwards came the whirlwind interview, infused with smiles and enthusiasm. He researched the business. It seemed solid, according to the information available. And now, the blessed offer beyond his wildest dreams had arrived… but too good to be true.

Damon checked his watch, too late in the day to call and accept. He sighed and microwaved his frozen dinner, then turned on the TV. He paid no attention, his mind swirled with visions of wealth and success.

Still, that gnawing feeling…

Damon climbed into bed, flicked off the light, and drifted off to sleep.

He stood in smoke, a thick white smoke. A soft breeze blew and dissipating the fumes revealed a headstone.

Nonplussed, he approached the gravestone. It was dark as onyx and reflected his own glimmering image on its smooth surface. Rugged letters etched the sepulchral mirror. He squinted, trying to the read the words inscribed, but they blurred in and out of focus. He reached out and traced his fingertips along the engraving. A ray of light beamed down upon the epitaph, and Damon distinguished only one word: PATSY.

"Whose grave is this?" he wondered.

"Yours," Grandpa whispered beside him.

Damon turned towards the voice, but saw only vapor.

"Too good…" the wind ululated.

Damon awoke with a start; dawn was peeping through the window-blinds.

He stared at the ceiling for a long time. Then he made a phone call.

Months later, the story exploded in the media. On the evening news, Damon watched as police handcuffed the company's newest employee. The poor idiot had accepted the offer Damon had declined.

"Honest work is never too good to be true," Damon stated, and switched off the TV.

The Message

The fire crackled in the fireplace and lit up the otherwise dusky room. Eric growled and dashed his glass of port against it. Flames flared and ashes swirled, giving Eric's reflection in the mirror above the mantel a grimace of abject fury. His thick eyebrows scowled and his teeth gnashed, as the flickering fire played with the lines on his face in a dance of light and shadow. He looked like a devil with the still-tender scar across his forehead and the gray hairs that now lined his face. Eric was young, but the war had aged him, and not well. He returned home with a permanent limp and a diminishing bank account. At least she had still been there … until now.

She ran off with Lewis, that lazy, two-timing blackguard who called himself a brother. Lewis knew nothing of brotherhood. Eric served with better men, far more valiant and loyal than his own flesh and blood. Meanwhile, Lewis spent the war flitting from party to party and squandering the rest of Father's fortune. Were he alive today, Father would tan Lewis's hide, no doubt!

Angry tears welled up in Eric's eyes, and snarling, he fought them back. They spilled down his cheeks anyway, and Eric wiped them away which such force his sleeve scraped his cheeks and the scar on his forehead stung. The fire rose and ebbed; he paced the room like a caged tiger, not heeding the searing pain in his leg, and clenching and unclenching his fist.

"Damn them!" He cursed at the walls, the rug, the mirror.

Tongues of fire licked his wrath as he glared into the fireplace. He ran his fingers through his hair and, in one swift move, up-ended the antique pedestal table by Father's old high-backed chair.

The baroque table had been one of Mother's favorite pieces of furniture. It had one ornate carved leg with a tripod base, a thick round tabletop with inlaid tile depicting a phoenix, and a tiny drawer that was always locked since the key had vanished before its arrival at the shop. The table rested on its side; the tiny drawer was now open, and a piece of paper lay on the rug beside it. The paper fluttered as the fire flickered, and Eric glared at it through gritted teeth and tear-filled eyes.

Curiosity crept up his spine, and Eric picked up the paper, which was folded into a letter with no recipient or sender. He broke the wax seal and opened it.

Eric huffed; gibberish. He was about to fling it into the fire when he gave it a second glance.

"This looks like a cryptogram," he muttered as he leaned closer to the firelight to read it.

Eric hobbled to Father's desk across the room, and sitting in the big leather chair, switched on the desk lamp. He reached for a pen, and with a nostalgic lump in his throat, set to decoding it as he had done years ago by Mother's sick bed. She loved puzzles and had bequeathed that love to him during many a peaceful evening. His last moments with her had been over a cryptic crossword he helped her decipher.

That skill served him well in the army, and he spent most of the war decoding messages from the Nazis to their Luftwaffe. Though he did not escape the bombs — the ghastly scar and his shattered leg proved it.

Eric focused his mind on the task at hand, forgetting her perfidy and Lewis's betrayal. A substitution code written in symbols, difficult, but not impossible.

The fire dwindled, and the room cooled around him, as the message appeared, letter by letter.

Confused, he furrowed his brow.

"Decipher this message and prosper for all eternity."

Eric leaned back in the chair and huffed.

"What is this?" He said, the fire hissed in reply.

Eric stood and, noting the chill, limped across the room and threw another log into the fire. The flames sputtered and cackled, playing with the dead wood.

Eric returned the overturned table to its upright position and sat on the high-backed chair beside it. He watched the flames crackle and pop as his eyelids grew heavy and drifted off to sleep. His hand drooped over the arm of the chair, and his fingers loosened the grip on the decoded message.

The paper fluttered on the rug as a draft of wind gusted through the room, despite the closed doors and windows. It lifted the paper into a whirlwind of dancing flames and blew it into the fire. With one final wheeze, the fire incinerated the cipher and died.

The cold crept into Eric's bones, and he stirred, shivering. He opened his eyes and stood to throw another log into the fire when, catching his reflection in the mirror, he gasped. The scar and the gray hairs had vanished! His youthful, flabbergasted face stared back at him, and only then did he realize he felt no pain in his leg. Rather, he felt no pain anywhere. He covered his mouth with his hand—a million thoughts flying through his brain—when he glanced into the cold hearth.

Glints and glimmers sparkled in the dim light of Father's desk lamp. Instead of glowing embers, Eric beheld a trove of diamonds, gold, silver and precious gems where only ashes should be.

On The Meadow

Darren lay on the meadow, pebbles sticking into his back through his T-shirt. He loved spending time among the trees and often felt he had a special connection with nature. Sometimes he thought the trees reached out to him, as if they wished to tell him a secret. He would then close his eyes and listen, but could never understand the message.

On this occasion, bathed in the warm sunlight, his mind was on the ground, wet and cool and lumpy. He breathed in the grass, the moss and damp earth. With closed eyes, he thought about the millions of feet that had walked upon the piece of dirt on which he lay. Animals, insects, birds and humans, how many had trampled here?

Minutes passed, and he noticed a slow and steady thumping; he opened his palm and touched the ground. It pulsed, thud, thud, thud, louder and stronger as if footsteps, big stomping footsteps approached. Darren opened his eyes, and a shadow fell across the pastel blue sky. He turned his head to one side just as a boot stomped beside his shoulder. Another plunked down by his hand.

Traipsing boots and gaiters soon engulfed Darren; the pungent scent of leather and mud stung. The ground shook with the footfalls, and the boom of the march so near his ears sounded like cannonballs. He lay motionless, heart racing, while above him the sky turned red, and a reeking cloud of wool, metal and gunpowder seared his nostrils.

As the boots marched away, Darren sat up and glimpsed the backs of British soldiers, their long red coats, muskets, bayonets and tricorn hats fading into the forest. Darren wanted to stand up and rush after them, but the sun was too bright and the heat weighed on him. He lay back down and closed his eyes.

The setting sun was casting an orange hue over the meadow when Darren awoke. He perked his ears and listened for footsteps, but heard nothing except the sounds of the evening forest. Darren walked home—his own footfalls loud in his ears—wondering whether the troop had been a dream or the specters of a long-dead reality.

Goodnight

The homeless man sat on the dingy stoop of the abandoned factory across the street from Rose's apartment building. She always saw him when she gazed out her bedroom window. The humpbacked figure sat beneath the street lamplight, as the night shadows danced around him.

To Rose, he was a sad figure, someone to pity, someone for whom to feel compassion. He never scared her, even when he looked up and stared at her window. He seemed to pierce the darkness and cast his gaze upon her. An instant later, his head would droop back down on his crooked shoulders. Rose knew he had not seen her, that he could not see through the double-paned window, into the darkened bedroom lit only by the faint reading lamp on the nightstand.

Every night, unseen, Rose would give the man a slight wave and tell him a silent goodnight as she switched off the lamp. He was always there, motionless, like a misshapen statue.

One night, as Rose's eyes searched the murk for the reassuring beam of light across the street, she noticed the hunched vagrant was not in his usual place.

Lightning flashed; thunder roared. A big storm was coming, and Rose hoped the drifter either made it to the safety of the tattered awning above the stoop, or had found decent shelter elsewhere.

Regardless, she gave the usual tiny wave and wished the hunchback goodnight as she turned off the light. She settled her head on her pillow, waiting for sleep and listening to the roaring storm.

Rose's eyes flew open. The storm had abated, and far away the sounds of tires driving on wet pavement shimmered in the silence of her apartment.

A sound had awakened her. A click, like the click of a deadbolt.

Rose's heart pounded as she kept still and listened to the darkness beyond the bedroom. Her hand slid out from under the covers and edged towards the nightstand, seeking her cellphone. Rose paled as her fingers touched only its wooden surface.

It's in the living room, she cursed herself as her pulse quickened.

Rose held her breath when she caught the distant sound of shuffling feet.

Despite the black overcast night, light peered through the window-grilles and Rose, frightened as she was, found it comforting.

Muffled footsteps approached her closed bedroom door.

She shifted her body towards the light glimmering through the window. From the height of the bed, Rose had a view of the abandoned factory and its stoop. There, in the lamplight, sat the humpbacked figure, and Rose's heart skipped with relief.

As unknown fingers closed around the bedroom doorknob, she was hyper-alert and comforted by the sight of the strange, yet familiar, vagabond across the street.

The doorknob turned; Rose stifled a sob and fixed her gaze on the slouching figure bathed in the golden ray of the street lamp.

The bedroom door inched open with a muffled squeak.

Rose's hand crept towards the window.

Help me, she implored in the same mind-voice she always bid the hunched tramp goodnight.

He looked up at her as if he heard her prayer. He glared at Rose's window and, for an instant, his eyes glowed with a silver spark.

Rose's spine crawled as the footsteps and presence of a big man approached her bed. Her fingers curled around the bedsheet as the sound of deep, lustful breaths reached her ears, and a human warmth inched towards her neck. Still, she kept her gaze fixed on the crooked beggar in the streetlamp.

The hunchback, his eyes still on the window, rose from the stoop. He rose and rose and rose until he stood straight and tall and powerful.

Rose's heart pounded.

A hand crept up her back and shoulder, then cupped her breast as the intruder lay down beside her. His hand wormed its way to her neck, feeling every inch of her clammy skin, and settled over her mouth.

"If you behave," the invader growled, "I won't kill you."

The radiant figure across the street entranced the immobile Rose, as a white pearlescent wing unfurled from its back, then another.

In a flash, the figure took flight, passed through the window-pane, and alighted on Rose's bed. It grabbed the screaming prowler by the neck and hurled him against the wall.

The prowler, frightened out of his wits, scrambled to stand while the angel stood tall and defiant with arms akimbo and wings splayed wide over Rose.

The intruder clutched at his face as if it burned, then tottered and clambered out the open bedroom door. Rose heard his frenzied screams as he bolted from the apartment and stumbled into the hallway. The inky gloom swallowed the manic would-be rapist as he floundered across the street, and his terrified yowls faded in the distance.

Soft, loving fingers now brushed Rose's cheek; she turned her head to meet the angel's gaze. His smile reached the golden-silver twinkle of his eyes. He kissed her forehead.

"Thank you," Rose murmured, but the angel had vanished.

As the fright ebbed, she gazed out towards the abandoned factory stoop. In the lamplight, she saw the comforting hunch-backed figure.

Rose gave her customary little wave and bid him goodnight.

Cat-O'-Nine-Tails

The abbess knocked on the door. The sounds of a flogging whip shook the darkened corridor; she received no reply. Starlight shone through the arched Gothic windows that lined the passage.

She knocked again.

Should she enter? The young novice needed the last rites.

The abbess knocked a third time and gave the door a slight push. It creaked open.

The bishop stood with his bare back to the door, and in the dim candlelight the abbess saw streaks of gooey blood marring the skin.

A whip cracked, and a wound opened.

What horrible sin could he be repenting?

Another crack and the pieces fell into place. As blood poured down the wounded back, images flowed through the abbess's mind. With each lash, she recalled every visit the bishop had made to her abbey and the events thereafter.

The young novice; the stillborn.

Sister Elizabeth; the drowning.

Her eyes widened, and the dreaded thought flashed like lightning: not coincidences, but consequences.

"You!" The abbess exclaimed; the bishop whirled around and glared.

She stood in the doorway, old, wrinkled and yet so innocent, but her wide eyes betrayed her horrible realization. The cat was out of the bag, his secret sins exposed.

He advanced towards her with such violence that she turned and ran; her frail steps booming with the guilt of his crimes. He followed down the narrow window-lined corridor, starlight and shadow alternating with each step. He caught her just as she reached the winding stone stairs.

They struggled; she scratched him. He tried to pull her back to his chamber, but she fought hard. To control those flailing arms, he pushed her. Her slight frame lifted off the floor, and, in an instant, she flew out the window.

The bishop glanced at the broken abbess pierced by the thorny briar and surrounded by shattered glass sparkling in the starlight. He returned to his chamber. A cat wailed in the night. Hurried footsteps.

Lillian gazed up from the book Derek had placed before her; eyes filled with fear and wonder. It had been blank, then little by little, the horrible scene had appeared within its pages, each moment ripped out of Lillian's mind like tangled hooks.

Derek took the book from her and wrapped it in its towel.

"Does this book show you your nightmares?" Lillian stammered.

"I don't know," Derek mumbled, "does it?"

ABOUT THE AUTHOR

Susana K. Marsch is fluent in English and Spanish. She worked in the financial industry in Boston, Massachusetts, but switched careers to do what she loves best: writing and art.

She is the author of *Rust: A Ghost Mystery Novel,* and now lives in San Antonio, Texas.

www.susanakmarsch.com

ALSO BY SUSANA K. MARSCH

Rust: A Ghost Mystery Novel

JACK'S DREAM HOUSE IS NOW HIS WORST NIGHTMARE…

Jack Adams has just bought the house of his dreams; it's perfect for him and offers him the peace and tranquility he seeks.

Too bad it's haunted.

The ghosts of the slain Jenkins family will not rest until their murderer is brought to justice.

Jack must now face his worst fear in his own home. He must find the killer to stop the haunting and bring peace to the souls of an entire family wiped out in cold blood.